ESCAPADES OF A PERSONAL STYLIST

Leanne Lovegrove

www.BOROUGHSPUBLISHINGGROUP.com

ESCAPADES OF A PERSONAL STYLIST
Copyright © 2021 Leanne Lovegrove

ISBN: 978-1-953810-15-1

To all those people who've chased their dreams

ACKNOWLEDGMENTS

A brief note of thanks to all the people who continue to support me in chasing my dreams.

And to you, dear reader: thank you most of all.

ESCAPADES OF A PERSONAL STYLIST

Chapter One

The tyres of Mrs Bennett's Porsche squealed on the pebbled driveway and Sophie braked hard. She over-steered the car to the left to avoid colliding with the manicured garden before coming to an abrupt stop.

She'd made it.

Unfamiliar with the prestigious suburb of Ascot, a long way out of her 'hood, and without the benefit of the GPS, she'd have been lost at the first turn out of the Brisbane CBD. Would probably be on her way to the Gold Coast instead.

Phew. Perhaps now her heart could stop beating so fast. Stress was her best friend, but today she had probably reached a new high.

But she wasn't in the clear yet. Best get on with it.

Wrenching the car door open, she glanced at her watch and a new wave of panic washed over her. No, she had this, but she needed to be quick. She kicked the door shut with one foot, extracted the house key from her bra and raced toward the mansion.

She opened the front door and it hit the entry wall with a thwack.

That hurt.

Slow down, Sophie.

But she couldn't. She wouldn't. The fashion show was due to commence at Customs House in thirty-five minutes.

Her stiletto heels clacked on the tiled floor as she strode toward the stairwell. She was headed to Mrs Bennett's bedroom on the second floor. But with one foot on the bottom step, Sophie paused.

She listened. She could have sworn she'd heard a deep, guttural groan. Like a man exerting himself.

Sophie whirled on the spot. A strand of hair came loose and she tucked it behind her right ear.

Silence echoed around the bright open space and she continued on, taking two steps at a time. Gold-framed paintings hung on the walls bordering the flight of stairs. Keeping her feet moving, she ignored the desire to stop and admire the intricate detail and colour of each piece. No one had told her that Mrs Bennett was an art enthusiast.

Whoa. Was that a Sidney Nolan? Mid-step, she paused to look.

No way. The Bennett's were more cultured than she'd given them credit for. Mega rich, but she'd already known that.

No time to be distracted by fabulous art, she had a job to do.

At the top of the stairs, she turned left, heeding the instructions that had been barked at her. The main bedroom would be at the end of the narrow hallway. She ploughed on down the corridor, tugging the long hem of her dress up with one hand to avoid tripping.

Nooo. Her ankle rolled to the left and she leaned against the wall to prevent falling. The four-inch heels she wore were not designed for walking fast. They were created for standing elegantly and still, or for sitting on bar stools and swinging a stiletto-clad foot for the wearer to be the subject of admiration. Sure, they were pretty, but right now she needed trainers.

Sophie gave her ankle a quick rub and hurried on. She'd deal with her aching feet later.

A glittering flash of light bounced off the white-washed walls and she spied a crystal chandelier through a gap in the door. It had to be the master bedroom. She raced faster and entered.

Holy shit.

Her hands flew up as she covered her eyes. With her lids locked shut, and her senses impaired, she tripped backward into the hard timber doorframe and dropped her hands.

A perky set of plump breasts bounced bang-on in her line of vision. A man kneeling behind the woman on her hands and knees thrust into her with calculated precision. His eyes were half-closed, his mouth open, and head rolled back wearing an expression of ecstasy.

Run or stay? Sophie's urge to flee pumped through her veins, but she couldn't. A pathetic whimper of indecision escaped her lips. Two pairs of eyes flashed open, neither wearing expressions of ecstasy now. Simultaneous shrieks and groans erupted from their wide-open mouths.

Like a scene in a movie, everything happened in fast forward. She'd not seen two people move so fast.

The man lunged backward landing on his bottom and the woman grappled for something to cover her naked body.

"Oh my God. I'm so sorry," Sophie muttered not knowing where to look. She glanced at the ceiling, the walls, and back to the floor to examine the carpet's intricate thread. Like everything else in the house, it was a variation of white, probably called snowflake or coconut or frost. "I, um, no one is supposed to be home. I'm here to collect Mrs Bennett's clothes for the fashion show," she rambled.

Neither spoke.

Sophie shuffled sideways toward the open wardrobe on the far side of the bedroom. In her peripheral vision, she saw the woman clutch the bed sheet to her chest and the man lean back onto the rumpled bed, remaining uncovered.

Said a lot.

Once safely inside the spacious walk-in-closet, she yelled, "Don't worry about me. I'll collect the clothes and be on my way. Won't take but a second."

Mrs Bennett's wardrobe spanned the rear of the room where a large quantity of dresses were hung with care. Sophie spotted a competitor's label.

"Oh, how could she?" she whispered, running her fingers along the sleek fabric and admiring the make and cut.

Lying over a chaise in the corner was the dress she'd been sent to collect. Sophie grasped the hanger and scanned the space quickly for accessories. Mrs Bennett had requested specific pieces to match the outfit. Where was the jewellery box? Sophie spied it in the recess of the open shelves and pounced on it and flipped the lid to search the contents.

The unmistakable sound of a zipper on a dress being slid up was followed by heavy footsteps. Then, a door slammed, echoing through the empty house.

How embarrassing to be sprung like that. Poor Mrs Bennett. Was that her husband having sex with someone who clearly wasn't his wife? Thoughts ricocheted through Sophie's brain as she rifled through an extensive collection of jewels searching for the sapphire and diamond set. Certainly, after having witnessed that scene, it seemed even more important to make her client happy. Finding the jewellery, Sophie clutched the set in her hand and cleared her throat before heading back into the bedroom. She slowed her pace when she really wanted to bolt right out of there. The inner voyeur in her, secretly wanting a stickybeak dared to peak at what the man and woman were doing now.

What does one do when they're busted having sex in the middle of the day with a person who isn't their spouse?

"I'll be on my way," she said to the man now dressed in a dark black suit standing next to the bedside table. His gold tie lay askew. He scrolled his phone and wore a look of disinterest, as if he didn't have a care in the world.

Bastard. Sophie grew angry on her client's behalf. What a creep.

Please don't talk to me, she willed, because she might say what she thought of him, and that would be all shades of disaster.

Dress in hand, her job done, all she wanted to get the hell out of there, and pronto.

He opened his mouth but Sophie hurried across the bedroom, ignoring him, but those darn heels caught in the plush carpet slowing her steps

The less she knew, the better. The woman had disappeared. Sophie left the bedroom and scooted down the stairs. A toilet flushed and muffled words echoed through the cavernous space.

"Gotta go, bye," Sophie sang out and slammed the front door shut.

She placed the dress and accessories in the rear of the Porsche and hopped into the driver's seat.

She had twenty-five minutes to deliver Mrs Bennett's ensemble before the models strolled down the catwalk featuring the latest range of Lilly Malone luxury fashions. Despite being as quick as she could in extreme circumstances, her client would unleash her wrath if she were tardy.

Mrs Bennett had to be kept happy. Sophie shook away the images of bouncing breasts and thrusting torsos, and together, with a fear of being late, she planted her foot on the accelerator. The hum of the Porsche gave her an unfamiliar satisfaction as she drove too fast.

Some days, she wished her job as a personal stylist was less exciting.

***

Max's phone vibrated as he sat at his dining room table. It was covered with crap: pens and pencils, dirty plates and mugs, tattered receipts, and discarded and unread newspapers. In slow motion, he glanced around the mess, happy to tear his gaze away from the papers in front of him.

Where was the stupid thing?

He could hear it, muted and dancing on the table. He was in no hurry to find it, because he didn't care who was on the other end.

Locating his phone under a notepad, he checked the screen. Sighing, he answered. "Hey, Luke. What can I do for you?"

"Max. I'm sick and I have a gig today." As if the effort of talking had exhausted his friend, Luke burst into robust coughing.

Max held the phone away from his ear until it stopped.

"Jeez, mate. You sound terrible. Is it the man-flu?" Max wasn't feeling sorry for him yet.

Luke attempted a laugh, but only croaked instead. "It's worse." he lamented. "But in all seriousness, this is a new contract today and I can't lose it. It's a reputable company who host a number of events throughout the year and if I stuff this up, it means a lot of lost dough. If I do well, it could lead to loads more work. That's always handy, right?" He coughed some more. "Actually, I'm bummed I can't do it because it's for some fancy fashion label. Apparently, highbrow, or so my sister tells me. She was impressed I'd landed it. Side bennie, this type of events means lots of attractive women wearing not a lot of clothes. What better way to spend an evening?"

Max bit his tongue. He could think of a hundred more attractive alternatives. Luke knew how Max felt and couldn't avoid ribbing him. Lucky he was a good friend. If he wasn't, he wouldn't have even answered the call.

But that didn't stop Max's stomach constricting. As usual with Luke, Max knew where this was heading. He decided to play dumb. "What's this news got to do with me? You need me to deliver some chicken soup to help you feel better?" The words came out flat, not like the jest he'd intended.

"Yeah, right, as if. Can you cover for me? It's good money, I can pay you cash. There's a few young blokes on to help you out, but you'll be in charge of the bar."

Max lifted up the sheaf of paper he'd been staring at when the phone buzzed. A tax invoice with bold red letters sprang out at him.

OVERDUE. He placed it back onto the burgeoning pile with the rest. In denial, he hadn't even glanced at them yet.

"I hate covering for you. These events are ghastly, rather than amazing, and a room packed with gorgeous woman is hideous and you know it. All the snobby rich people of Brisbane in one place," Max groaned down the phone. "The women might be beautiful, but they've got the attitude to match. You know the sort. No doubt, they all have rich boyfriends, anyway." Max paused to let his words sink in.

Truth be told, he wouldn't refuse. He'd do the job but couldn't help the whinge before he agreed.

"Get it, mate. But it's my business, and we only have to be experts at pouring the drinks. It's not hard. You need to relax a little, go with it. You might actually enjoy yourself. Plus, I wouldn't ask if I wasn't desperate. I'd get Pete, but he's at his brother's wedding."

Max's eyes roamed back over to the notice. Cash was exactly what he needed right now. This job would assure him he could pay his rent this week, and that would be one less bill. One less stress. No point having a toddler tantrum about it.

"Damn it, Luke. You owe me. Give me the details."

"You're a legend, and yeah, I owe you. Only thing is, you need to get going now, it starts at three. I'll text you the address and the names of the blokes who'll be helping you."

"What's the time now?" Max launched out of his chair, turned his phone over to look at the time, and cursed. Five minutes after two. "Mate, you serious? Couldn't you've let me know any later? Man. I have to shower and get out of my work gear. I stink. Thanks for the late notice."

Max shut down the call to Luke's chuckles, then coughing spasm.

At least in his rush, he didn't have time to think about what was ahead.

Chapter Two

Sophie sank down into the leather seat of the Porsche and imagined she was a formula one driver, hugging the bends in the road and hurtling so fast, no one could catch her. Her foot itched to press down further on the accelerator, but damn, she couldn't do it.

Lost in her fantasy, she entered the car park short and careened over a parking barrier. At the loud clunk, she gripped the steering wheel and her knuckles turned white.

Calm the hell down, Sophie and stop daydreaming.

God forbid it was necessary, Mrs Bennett could afford the repair, but that wasn't the issue. Sophie losing her job through stupidity was, and that was not an option. The mere prospect of unemployment had a light sheen of sweat breaking out on her brow. If Lilly Malone lost one of their most lucrative clients, Sophie would be a goner. She couldn't even entertain the idea.

What had gotten into her? Must be because she missed lunch. Now that she thought about it, she did feel a little light-headed.

She paused and concentrated on pushing deep breaths of air into her lungs. Once her pulse had stopped beating in her ears, she inched the car forward carefully until she spotted a convenient parking spot and maneuvered the Porsche to a smooth stop.

Only a few minutes remained until showtime.

Sophie reached for the packages in the rear and bundled them all into her arms. She exited the car with legs first and rose up tall without looking.

And bang, ran straight into a brick wall.

"What the hell?" came a deep growl.

Sophie peered around the travel bag she held aloft and was greeted with a serious face set into a scowl.

Okay, not a brick wall. The bulky hard surface of a man. A tall, broad man.

He held a tray of glasses that teetered in his grasp. Before the bundle crashed to the ground, he righted the tray and held it steady. Slate-grey eyes bored into her. Sophie watched his pulse beat out of his neck and his jaw clench tight.

A dark smattering of facial hair lined the man's square chin. A low cap shaded his face. Sophie wanted to apologise for bumping into him, but she'd gone mute. It was as though he'd stolen her tongue. She didn't know what was going on in her chest, but it felt like her heart was going to explode right out its safe cavity.

"You've parked too close to my car. I can't unpack my equipment." The guy spoke like he held his body-stiff and unmalleable.

Now that she was paying attention, their bodies were crushed close together in between the parallel vehicles. So close, her arm brushed his warm skin, and neither of them could move. Well, she could, if he backed up to where he'd come from.

Sophie glimpsed down into the interior of the old Datsun next to her. Detritus was strewn across the back seat. There were used coffee cups, boxes, takeaway litter, and maybe an assortment of clothes or perhaps old rags. It was a disgusting mess. Sophie reflex gagged. She turned her gaze back to the guy invading her personal space. One look, and she could tell he'd read her expression.

His eyes narrowed so she couldn't see their colour anymore, and he lifted his chin.

She spoke before he could. "I'm in a rush to deliver these clothes inside, but I promise, I'll come back and move the car. I'll be as fast as I can." Sophie stepped forward but he blocked her path.

Move she wanted to scream at him.

As if he'd heard her exclamation, the man back stepped toward the rear of his vehicle and opened the boot. There was the rattling of wheels and someone arrived with a trolley to assist him unload. He ignored her now as if she didn't exist.

She wanted to stab his foot with her stiletto heel. It took all her willpower to hold her leg steady as she stepped forward. So rude. She'd said sorry, hadn't she?

Damn it. She hadn't, no wonder he was pissed.

No time to worry about any of that now, she had to deliver Mrs Bennett's outfit. She'd come back and make amends. Shift the car, whatever.

She marched down the narrow stretch between their vehicles and looked ahead to the entry door only metres away. Her priority was protecting the dress and not dropping the satchel of jewellery and shoes.

Her entire line of sight was restricted but she didn't have far to go. She took two steps and her toes kicked something on the ground sitting next to the Datsun. It toppled and cracked before glass shattered at her feet. She smelled spice and fruit and heard bubbles popping before liquid soaked her shoes. Champagne? Oh no, what a waste.

"Oh my gosh, I'm so sorry. I didn't see it, I couldn't, didn't know it was there…" she mumbled and swallowed the profanity that threatened. Why was that stupid bottle on the ground anyway?

Datsun-man stood beside her but did not offer to help. His face turned puce as he surveyed the damage. A dull ache came from behind her temples and throbbed.

"Can you please go away?" he asked.

"Let me help." But she really didn't mean it. A disaster loomed if she didn't get on her way. What else could go wrong before she got inside?

"What? And damage your designer dress?" He smirked. His derisive tone cut, but matched the sneer and disdain etched on his face. Standing up taller, she held in the tears on the brim of escaping down her cheeks and walked away as steadily as she could so as to avoid any further accidents. At least she still held onto Mrs Bennett's belongings.

Prick. Who the hell was this guy anyway, and why did he make her heart race?

***

Max knew he shouldn't have accepted this job.

He brushed up the glass shards and swept them into the dustpan. The tiniest sliver pierced his thumb and a blood droplet formed. He sucked on it quickly before it could stain his white shirt.

Goddamn that woman with her pale, porcelain skin and almond eyes. Bet she relied upon those looks to get out of all sorts of scrapes. Some people had the world in their hands, didn't they? Max yanked a box from the boot.

Adrenalin pumped through his chest and it constricted. Why was he so agitated? Good luck to that woman and her exquisite beauty and her European car and designer clothes. Was she researching a cure for cancer in her spare time? Probably not. That meant she was no better than him.

"She was pretty hot, wasn't she?" the young waiter said as he sidled up next to the Datsun to carry the next crate. The guy wore the trademark black and white of hospitality but his hair was long and tousled, the only part of him expressing any of his personality. He grinned wide, as if ready to eat the woman.

"Sure was," Max agreed. How could he not? "Think she's in your league?"

The smart comment was met with a shrug.

"You're dreaming," Max said and turned away.

Chapter Three

Sophie lurked in a corner of the conference room desperate to avoid Mrs Bennett. They'd been no time for pleasantries after she'd delivered the outfit earlier. She'd gotten only quickly proffered thanks.

Of course, now, an hour later, her luck ran out, and worse, her husband hung off Mrs Bennett's arm.

"Sophie, darling. Thank you for rescuing me earlier." Audrey Bennett clung to her husband. "Frank, this is my personal stylist, Sophie Williams. She saved my skin tonight by rushing back to the house and collecting this dress." She flounced the skirt for effect. "The one I was wearing ripped at the bust." Audrey giggled like a schoolgirl, but Sophie noticed Mr Bennett's stiff stance.

"You did take a rather long time, darling. I was beginning to worry. What kept you?"

Sophie stared at Frank. He wore a vacant expression. Empty. Flat. Not a flicker of emotion crossed his face. She tried not to imagine him naked and out of his suit. She'd seen way more of him than she wanted. Instead, she focused on her client.

"I hit the school traffic on my way back into town." Sophie shrugged. "But don't you look amazing. I was so happy to help. There were many wonderful designs on display tonight that would suit you perfectly. Perhaps your husband will let you order the entire collection?" Sophie caught him in a steely stare before walking away.

***

Max tried hard to be on his best behaviour. He was doing this for Luke and his business, after all. Luckily Max wasn't being paid based on the number of smiles he doled out.

As a remittance to his friend and punishment to himself, he'd worked relentlessly, not even stopping for a break. His limbs were heavy from carrying trays laden with glasses, pulling beers, and popping corks. It'd been a while since he'd been on his feet for so many hours, but he quelled any complaints as soon as the thoughts arose. He'd felt sorry for himself too much lately, and he was over it. Yet, it was difficult keeping his agitation at bay.

It didn't help that the image of the too-skinny, tall klutz of a woman wouldn't leave his mind. God, she'd infuriated him. He'd overreacted, but he kept telling himself he could care less about her, her social status, or her fancy car.

Tonight many women had grasped his bottom, fluttered their eyelashes, and even attempted to pass him their room keys. If only he was a different sort of bloke. He could've had endless fun with these women who didn't know how he voted, his view on gun control, or whether he was actually a nice guy. One day soon he'd take advantage of their guileless natures and he'd bloody well enjoy it.

Rolling his shoulders back to release the tension, he recalled the crazy fashion he'd witnessed on the runway. It'd given him a number of ideas for abstract sculptures and he couldn't wait to jot them down when he returned home. The colours had been hypnotic and the distressed fabrics had turned his mind to timber and how he might create some innovative designs. At least these ideas gave him a buzz. Loving that feeling, he noticed a spring in his step. Maybe these ideas would convert to a new range of sculptures, something different, something groundbreaking. Or perhaps his excitement grew because his shift was nearing the end. Not too long now and he'd collect his cash for the rent and drive fast, away from the over-ripe smell of excess money.

On cue, another customer approached the bar. He wiped the bench one last time before placing the cloth in his back pocket. The woman at the bar faced the dwindling crowd but turned toward him as she read her wrist watch. A frown creased her forehead as she read the time.

Her.

Max waited for her drink order. If he had to guess, he'd say champagne would be her choice. Some of the bottles he'd served tonight would've paid his bills for the next month.

She'd changed her clothes since their encounter in the car park. He'd thought the previous get-up was fancy, but this was much more elaborate and most likely, much more expensive. Now, she wore a long, chiffon emerald-green dress without sleeves and it had a matching scarf of the same material gathered at her neck. Her dark locks were swept up into a bun. Was the fabric like her: soft and nice to the touch?

She turned. "Oh, hello." Her voice wavered with uncertainty.

His gaze roamed her chest. The dress had a neat V cut, allowing plump exposed flesh to tantalise him. His mouth dried and he licked his lips then swallowed and forced his gaze up. Her make-up accentuated her features, and the subtlety of the green turned her dark eyes black. Those eyes searched his. With her long fingers, she swept a solitary strand of hair away from her face and placed it behind her right ear. Her ears were adorned in bling. The silence continued and she cleared her throat and shifted slightly on her feet.

Vulnerability oozed off her. Puzzled, Max studied her. He had to be reading the signs wrong. This woman fitted perfectly into this pack of pampered princesses as well as any other he'd served tonight. The clothes, the jewellery, and of course, the Porsche from earlier, spelled rich.

The background music that'd played throughout the evening ceased, the silence pulling him from his trance. Max shook his head trying to return his common sense as he balled his fists tight by his side. Forget her beauty, she'll be like the rest of the glitterati that crammed into the function room.

"What would you like?"

"Um, a vodka and orange please."

Okay, he'd been wrong. Only kids who couldn't handle their alcohol drank this concoction.

Without speaking he poured her request and served it in a fine crystal glass. She checked her watch again. She lifted the drink and sucked on the straw to down half the contents. Max was transfixed on the rosebud lips surrounding that straw, and then his gaze moved to her throat as she swallowed. In another gulp, she'd drained the drink and returned it to the counter. Ignoring him, she pulled out her phone and punched out a message and frowned with pursed lips that remained moist.

"I assume you'd like another?"

Turning her attention away from her phone, she considered him like she'd forgotten he was there. "Yes, please."

Max placed the second drink on the bar and another woman approached, dressed in a ridiculous outfit that resembled one of those toilet roll dollies that his grandmother used to sit on the top of her cistern. It was the same bright yellow of his memory but wasn't knitted or crocheted. He could never tell the difference. The dress was one big ruffle. It sat in waves across the woman's bust and down the full length skirt with the only reprieve from all that material being a large split revealing one leg. He noticed the wearer had to keep a firm grip on each side of the dress to control it and allow her to walk freely. Who bought this stuff?

The woman drinking vodka and orange didn't seem to notice the crazy get-up. Obviously such extraordinary clothing was usual in her world. Hands gesticulated in the air and smiles were exchanged as they engaged in what he imagined was frivolous small talk. The vodka and orange snuck one last glance at her phone before placing it back in her clutch. Her hand reached for the glass and she checked her watch again.

Not his problem if her boyfriend was late. Perhaps he'd park his Lamborghini next to her Porsche. Max stacked the glasses and his eyes kept flicking back to the beauty in the green dress. His groin quivered. He ignored it and the possibility that she might be different. He hadn't been with a woman in months and it was simply his hormones in overdrive.

He'd have to fix that soon.

Chapter Four

Sophie closed the door to her apartment softly behind her, leaned against it and released a heavy sigh.

Home. Now she could relax.

The entire time she performed her job as a personal shopper—or as some preferred to call themselves, a *stylist*—for Lilly Malone Luxury Fashion Label, she was an actress playing a part for which she'd never auditioned. The charade exhausted her.

She kicked off her shoes. Thanking the cool tiles for soothing her throbbing soles, Sophie headed down the short hall to her sister's room. A dim light escaped under Gaby's doorframe despite it being after midnight.

"Hey, I'm home," Sophie said after knocking lightly and entering the room. Her sixteen-year-old sister sat in bed with books spread across her doona, pencil stuck between her teeth and a frown on her forehead.

Gaby smiled and Sophie's heart hitched. This was why she worked so hard at a silly job. She loved her sister more than anything in the world. She leaned down and kissed the top of Gaby's head.

"I'm sorry I'm so late. I texted but you didn't respond, I thought you were asleep. Why are you still up?"

"I know. Sorry, I didn't see your message. I've got a bit carried away with this English assignment, I need to proof it, but it can wait until tomorrow."

"Good idea. I'll read through it then. Is this the one about the Greek gods?" Out of nowhere an image of the belligerent barman flashed into Sophie's mind. He did look a bit Greek, or maybe Italian, with his dark wavy hair that was too long and met the beard that covered his chin. She bet that face would be gorgeous without all that hair. Sophie smiled, *no,* it was attractive just as it was.

"Why are you smiling?" Gaby asked, her bright face shining through the muted light.

"Oh, nothing." Sophie giggled. "I might have seen a Greek god tonight. He had the looks, and probably the aggression and ego of one of those mythical creatures. Who was the leader of them all? Is it Zeus? No, Thor."

"Sophie." Her sister swatted her arm playfully. "He's a superhero. Maybe this guy is Eros. You know, the god of love and attraction?"

A handful of butterflies released in Sophie's tummy at the childish talk. "Don't be silly. Now get to sleep. Would you like a hot chocolate to help you settle?"

"I'd love that. Thanks, Soph."

At the door to Gaby's room, Sophie turned back. "Are you feeling okay?"

"Of course, I'm fine."

That was a relief, for now. Before she exited, Gaby spoke again. "Sophie, do you remember what today is?"

Sophie scratched her forehead and scrunched up her eyes. She was so tired it hurt to think. Then the date sprang into her addled brain and tears blinded her eyes. Putting her hand to her mouth, she hurried back to Gaby and hugged her tight.

"Can you believe Mum and Dad have been gone for five years?"

Sophie nodded.

"It's been so long. I'm struggling to remember what they look like and recall memories of time we spent together. It's getting worse every year."

"But that's why photos are so fabulous, right? We have so many great shots of them, of all of us."

"Yep, you're right. But it's gonna always hurt, isn't it?"

"Yep, sure is. I'll get our drinks."

With her heart now sitting heavy in her chest, Sophie turned on the lights in the small kitchen to make their hot chocolates. She held onto the fridge door and stretched her back and eased out the kinks. Her body hurt and her limbs were sore, but worst of all was the ache that spread across her breastbone. The inside of her chest cavity felt hollow and empty. It should have been filled to capacity with the love of her family.

How could she have forgotten the anniversary of her parent's death?

Unforgiveable.

Even if she had been working twenty-four seven this week, and today had been all-consuming with the latest launch show, she should've remembered. There was no excuse, particularly when Gaby needed her. Sophie's throat thickened, and the guilt sat there in a hard lump.

The creamy chocolate milk would help. Sophie grimaced as she peered into the fridge: the shelves were bare. She lifted out the half-empty milk bottle and removed the lid and smelled. All okay. Thank goodness it wasn't off. Hadn't she been to the grocery store? It felt like she spent most of her spare time there. She stretched into the far reaches of her brain to remember what day it was.

Friday. She hadn't been shopping all week because she'd been so busy at work. She'd shop tomorrow. Bugger, she could have devoured an entire tub of cookies and cream ice cream right now.

Out of nowhere, her eyes throbbed and all she wanted to do was close them and go to sleep. Her shoulders slumped. Here was her old nemesis grief, come back to haunt her. Like usual, she flicked an internal switch and concentrated on Gaby. Nothing else mattered. Gaby anchored her. Gaby needed her, and Gaby's care was Sophie's only purpose. To care for her sister through her illness and take the place of their parents. That was what was important.

After making the drinks, she crept back into Gaby's room and slipped into bed beside her. Together they drank and cuddled and talked of better, happier times. Even after Gaby had drifted off to sleep, Sophie lay there contemplating what the future would hold, sleep forgotten. Despite loathing her job, she was grateful for the work and chastised herself for forgetting that.

Fatigue, that was all it was. She needed this job and would do whatever it took to keep it.

Sleep caught up with her, and a rude strange man she didn't even know kept popping into her mind.

Chapter Five

"Good morning, honey." Inez trilled as Sophie entered the offices of Lilly Malone. "Looks like you had a wild weekend. Good on you, sweetie." Inez, CEO and Queen Bee of Lilly Malone was always happy.

God, if only she knew. No one at Sophie's place of employment had any idea about her personal life, and certainly not about her dependent sister, and they never would. Sophie wouldn't risk her job by sharing her predicament, but living a lie was awfully hard work. She suppressed her sigh.

Eight-thirty on Monday morning, and with the same energy she wrapped herself in her designer clothes, she fixed into place the façade that became Sophie Williams, personal shopper. She transformed from a grungy old moth to a beautiful butterfly, all with the help of her chic clothes and carefully applied makeup.

Her choice today was all about comfort. Not that she'd admit it, but she loved the dress she wore. It was old, in fashion years anyway. A dress released summers ago. No one else working at Lilly Malone would be seen dead in it because it was passé by now. Too soon since its release to be vintage or retro. It was flowy and loose, yet striking with a dark green cotton that displayed a flamboyant flower pattern swirled around the base. A few flowers crept up and appeared on the long sleeves. Wearing this outfit Sophie felt all woman. God knew, she needed that super power today.

It was the attitude to match that was more difficult to concoct when she least felt like it.

Even layers of concealer couldn't hide the pillows of pale, puffy skin that lined her eyes this morning. Their late night visit to the hospital had meant little sleep for either her or Gaby. She'd left Gaby sleeping off the effects of the all-nighter, but unlike her baby sister, she couldn't spend the day in bed. Work beckoned, as always.

That's okay. Gaby was well now, her sugar levels back to normal, and that was all that mattered. Sophie offered a silent prayer of thanks.

"I have the best news for you on this fabulous Monday." Inez flapped her hands in excitement and the bangles on her arms jingled.

Sophie garnered her strength to appear intrigued and plastered the smile on her face. "Ooh, how exciting. Tell me." Her words came out flat, not matching her boss's mood.

Inez regarded her quizzically, but was interrupted by a call.

Sophie waited and her mind twirled with possibilities of what the exciting news might be. Whatever it was, as one of the most talented employees of the label, she would do her best to be amazed. After Inez disconnected, she turned her attention back to Sophie.

"Annabelle is sick, and Mrs Heilbronn, you know of Malibu Coffee fame, needs an entire summer holiday wardrobe flown over to her in Morocco." Inez sang the last word. "You have a VIP new client appointment this morning and then you must go home and pack. You fly out tonight." The pitch of Inez's voice rose until it was almost a squeal. Her boss had no trouble exhibiting her exhilaration.

Shit.

Sophie knew what she had to do. "Oh my God. That's fantastic, Inez, thank you. That cannot compare to my wild weekend. Morocco, how exotic. How long will I be away?"

"A week, honey. Fly out tonight, you'll be back by Friday in time for next weekend. We don't want to work you too hard, do we?"

Double shit.

"That's unreal." She turned to go, having trouble keeping up the pretence because her stomach swirled. "I need a coffee before getting started. I'm heading downstairs, want one?"

"Yes please, darling. You know how I like it. A small double shot, three-quarter almond milk with extra froth and a sprinkling of chocolate."

"Got it. Be back in a jiffy." Sophie strode from Inez's office, stepping over the boxes of hats and scarfs and animal-patterned fabric ready for next season's designs, and quietly shut the door behind her.

Keeping her head low to avoid eye contact with any of the other staff, she walked through the plush plum offices with deep-pile carpet, extravagant chandeliers, and expensive paintings. With a sigh, she pulled out her mobile phone.

This situation called for an emergency call to elderly Mrs Miller who lived in the flat above them on level three. Sophie didn't travel a lot–though it felt like it–but when she did, Mrs Miller always checked on Gaby. At sixteen, her sister could look after herself, but Sophie felt anxious leaving her alone. Please let Mrs Miller be home this week and not away at a bowls tournament. Anxiety tangled her gut as the phone rang.

Mrs Miller answered as Sophie waited in the café queue. Mrs Miller was home and able to help. All would be okay. World order was briefly restored.

The smell of coffee permeated the air and Sophie sucked up the aroma and kept her calm. When she took her first sip, she closed her eyes. The caffeine quietened the adrenalin pulsing through her body. She took three more sips quickly before the elevator delivered her back to the tenth floor of Lilly Malone.

Sophie breathed deeply and slunk back into Inez's office.

"Here you go. I'll drink this and head out to visit my new client. It'll be great to have someone else on my books. Do you know much about her?"

Inez gestured for Sophie to sit and they drank their hot drinks as Inez briefed her on the newest VIP to join the ranks.

***

Sophie drove the company BMW coupe, a prestige car always gave the impression of importance, that whoever was driving was someone with a purpose. Sophie was grateful for the wheels because she didn't have her own car. Another expense she didn't need.

The GPS announced her arrival, and Sophie glanced out of the passenger seat window towards the house.

Inez had shared that Mrs Cartwright was a successful real estate agent. Her boss had neglected to mention filthy rich. The dazzling white house stood three stories high with bay windows, Greek style columns at the entry, and immaculate gardens where not even a stray leaf was evident.

Oh my gosh, is that a tennis court? Sophie leaned forward to gain a better view. Yep. Indeed it was. Sitting adjacent to the home was a fenced in full court.

This is going to be fun.

Sophie lugged out her catalogues, fabric samples and laptop, and her heels clicked up the pebble path passing an elaborate water fountain playing operatic music.

"Hello, Mrs Cartwright. I'm Sophie Williams from Lilly Malone, how are you today?" she said as the door opened. Too late, the lady dressed in a black skirt and white top smiled shyly at her mistake.

Inside, her gaze was immediately drawn to the glass atrium above. A brilliant cloudless sky filled her vision. It was so striking she forgot she was inside. The see-through ceiling filled the room with natural light. All the bright, white surfaces dazzled like they were illuminated. Sophie squinted. What was it with rich people and white?

She gulped. She might be in a different league here.

"Mrs Cartwright will be down in a minute." The maid scampered out of the living room.

Moments later, a woman entered clasping an earring to her lobe. The sparkles on her ears matched the diamonds around her neck. In the middle of a chain of jewels sat a bright, red ruby, which complemented her powder blue crisp suit and matched the matte shade of her lipstick. Atop her head sat a pair of glasses hidden amongst a neatly-pinned French roll.

Impressive. Sophie had seen all nature of ostentatiousness before, and after working for Lilly Malone for five years, appearances did not faze her. Instead, she saw dollar signs. A wealthy client equalled a good payday for Sophie, and Mrs Cartwright was all hers.

Sophie stood and extended her hand and immediately launched into her proven spiel about how Mrs Cartwright couldn't possibly require a personal stylist. Inevitably, that was always met with a low chuckle of delight. Flattery worked.

After an hour, Mrs Cartwright was her new best friend. Sophie wrapped up after receiving an endless list of requests that could easily be ordered back at HQ.

"Oh, and one last thing. A couple of years ago Lilly Malone produced a shoe, a dress sneaker, in fact, that had pink jewels along its edge and a delightfully colourful tread." Mrs Cartwright stared at

Sophie who rapidly blinked back at her. Little sweat droplets formed in the dip of her breasts.

Oh yes, she knew exactly what Mrs Cartwright referred to. They were a fabulous seller and an exclusively limited edition. One hundred pairs had been created, never to be produced again. Sophie wracked the far recesses of her brain to scan for information about whether they had more designer shoes coming out? She'd memorised the latest summer catalogue and nothing came to mind.

Do not ask for a pair.

"Yes, they were ever so wonderful," Mrs Cartwright went on. "My friend, Beatrice at the tennis club has a pair and I'm so disappointed I didn't know about them at the time. But, of course, now that I'm an exclusive customer working directly with you, I would like a pair."

A personal stylist's job was to make the impossible happen: locate and deliver the hard-to-buy products, those sought after and talked about at A-list parties. Anything was usually possible for the right price. But this, without even asking, Sophie was pretty sure that this, she couldn't deliver.

All her hard work from the last hour crashed around her. If she went back to Inez and the new VIP client had folded, no... She couldn't even contemplate it. Of course, an image of her sister popped into her mind, the ever-present reminder of why she performed so well at this job and had to work hard always. Sophie knew that Gaby required more insulin and had her next endocrinologist appointment coming up. Both expensive despite the subsidies provided. Not for the first time Sophie wished Australia had completely free healthcare.

She formed the words to reply but the front door slammed. It brought with it a gust of wind strong enough to make Sophie's hair lift. A distraction. Thank goodness. Mrs Cartwright turned away, and Sophie snuck in a breath and wiped her sweaty palms on her skirt.

"Hello, Maximilian, do you have it?" A clipped tone had infiltrated Mrs Cartwright's voice.

A tall man with wide shoulders entered the room carrying something so bulky and awkward that he walked slightly hunched over. "Yeah, here it is," he said.

The object covered in bubble wrap was slowly and carefully placed on the closest table.

The man hadn't noticed Sophie sitting on the chaise. Any minute she expected him to whip out a delivery note and have Mrs Cartwright sign. Instead, he took meticulous care unwrapping it.

"Don't do that, Maximillian. Leave it encased. It has to be delivered to Diane's office anyway, best to keep it protected."

"Don't you want to see it?" The man's words came out strangled as though his private parts were being squeezed. Maximillian had a deep, masculine voice. A voice that commanded attention. He was sort of rude though to Mrs Cartwright, unnecessarily abrupt.

Sophie stared at him and a prickle of apprehension crept up her spine.

Chapter Six

Sophie fanned her hot cheeks and lifted her sweaty legs off the leather couch to provide them with some cool air.

This guy was familiar. That voice, those mannerisms…

Then, as though she'd shouted and had drawn attention to herself, he turned. His face, that short beard, those eyes… OMG. He was the rude barman, aka Greek god, from the event the other night.

What was he doing here? Did he moonlight as a courier driver, too?

"No, not now. I'm in the middle of something."

His shoulders slouched at Mrs Cartwright's words and he gazed lovingly at the object he'd delivered. Then he straightened. "Okay. Do you have the payment?" He'd matched her words with his own clipped, officious tone.

"No. That has nothing to do with me. You need to speak to Diane—"

He lifted his palm and held it up to her face, not allowing her to finish. "Agreement was payment upon delivery."

Mrs Cartwright glared and he scowled right back. Tension hung in the air and no one spoke.

Um, okay, awkward. Sophie jumped up and went over to examine the object. She lifted one corner of the tape to peek at the contents inside.

The man was by her side in a second. "Do you mind?"

She'd heard a similar phrase before.

"Oh, not at all. What is it?" Sophie held the plastic wrap, but he placed his large, workman hand on top of hers, preventing her from unwrapping the package further.

Sophie jerked her hand away with rocket speed. His touch didn't send a shock of electricity pulsing through her, but instead a lightning bolt that slammed right up her arm. A delicious shudder heated her body.

Maximilian felt it too, if the widening of his eyes was any indication. His brows arched haughtily. Unlike her lightning speed reaction, his hand hovered in place, floating over the object as if he was confused. His features relaxed, and his gaze upon her was like a soft caress. Seconds passed before he pulled his hand back to his side.

Mrs Cartwright spoke again and the bubble encasing them burst. "Well, if that's how you're going to be, you'll have to deliver it yourself to her personally at the agency. I believe you know her address." She turned away from him and addressed Sophie.

"I believe we are also concluded. I trust you'll be able to confirm my order for the designer sneakers in addition to all the other items we discussed." The words hung in the air and the room became electrified. Mrs Cartwright waited for Sophie to react before giving a curt smile and leaving the room.

Holy shit, Sophie had forgotten about the shoes. She had to control her foot from stamping into the plush carpet.

"You know her?" he sneered the words. He was back to his usual self after their *moment.*

This guy was weird.

Sophie shrugged. "Yes. I'm her new personal stylist from Lilly Malone." For once, stylist seemed entirely appropriate.

Nodding his head, his forehead lost its creases as his face cleared.

"Lilly Malone. Didn't they have an event the other night? What was it, Friday night?" he asked and added, "And were you there?"

"Yep. I recognise you. You work in hospitality and do deliveries as a courier?" she asked.

His eyes focused intently on the package. It didn't appear as if he heard her. If he had, he ignored her question.

Instead, he pulled out his mobile phone and punched out a message. It pinged immediately and he flung it aside and blew air into his cheeks making them puff out. He ran his hands through his hair.

Broad shoulders heaved as he breathed. He was so close, so masculine, Sophie couldn't wrench herself away. A delightful shiver ran through her body remembering his touch. Her mouth hung open, and she shut it and wiped her chin with the back of her hand in case drool had escaped.

He moved, and her spell broke and dropped her dramatically back to Earth. Enough daydreaming about Mr Maximilian. She moved to gather her belongings. The sun was high in the midday sky, and she needed to pack for Morocco. How ridiculous those words sounded.

Plus, she needed to find a miracle solution to the designer shoes that were exclusive and no longer available. Another one of those stress headaches formed behind her eyes. Her head was constantly throbbing.

"Okay, I've gotta go." Sophie stood with her hands full and moved to the entry. He still gazed at the package, as if wishing it would come to life.

Slowly, he turned to her and stepped into her path. She couldn't read his face but his pulse throbbed in his neck again like Friday night.

Uh oh. Did she do something wrong?

"I hate to ask, but can you give me a lift?"

"Um, okay."

"My friend dropped me over here, but he's at work now and can't return. I need to deliver this." He pointed to the object. A flush crept across his cheeks.

"You need a lift with that?"

Now it was his turn to shrug.

***

Sophie left to place her gear in the car. Max listened for any sound of his mother. Had she gone to retrieve his money? Trust her not to have payment. She knew it was important. It had taken three long months to complete this piece, and for her friend, no less. He cocked his ear, again, hopeful. Nothing.

Unforgivable, but he'd come to expect nothing less.

His mother would do anything to force him to comply and to admit he'd been wrong. In a grovel, if he admitted he was rash, ridiculous, and/or stupid, his mother would accept any of those apologies. He understood his family's disappointment, but what his mother and father underestimated was his determination. Some might call it stubborn, but he was driven. He wouldn't give in. He'd starve before he gave them the satisfaction.

His mother had threatened to cut him out of the family after he'd quit his job at a top accounting firm and announced he wanted to be an artist. If he remembered correctly, his mother had scoffed at first. She'd longed for it to be a joke, but one look at Max's face told her it was real. Then the anger and retribution commenced.

Max was cut off and cut out. Not one nod of understanding. Not one line of encouragement. Not one dollar to support his aspirations. Once he left his six-figure salary behind, he was on his own. Of course, he could live here in their house with his parents. *Ugh.* His gaze swept the opulent home. If he stayed, he'd be here on their terms. Nope. The luxury wasn't worth it. Their terms didn't suit him.

Except for one minor problem, He was broke. Which brought him back to his current dilemma.

Predictably, his mother had disappeared into the caverns of the house and left him to sort out getting paid. She could've given him the money and got it from Diane, but no. His mother was hellbent on making his life as difficult as she could. She figured he'd cave and return to a profession, salary and lifestyle she and his father found acceptable. *Think again, mommy dearest.*

The front door slammed and the woman returned to the living room.

Her.

It was convenient she was here, but Max couldn't quite figure her out. Was she one of her mother's minions, or worse, an assistant parading as a rich, snobby type, or something in between?

He wished he didn't care. But here, they'd crossed paths again and out of her designer cocktail wear, she was different. Today she wore some crazy hippy-looking dress that flowed around her legs and had over-sized flowers on the skirt. It looked like an outfit that belonged at Woodstock. But it didn't look ridiculous. She glowed, had a presence and an aura that intrigued him.

She was like a ray of sunshine that cracked through a cover of grey clouds and the room brightened. He took a step back. She was alluring. Observing her, with sudden clarity, he understood why. She was unaware of her beauty and charm. Of the classic features that most women yearned to have. High cheekbones with well-spaced eyes in an oval face. Her dark eyes and hair stood in stark relief to her blemish-free, pale porcelain skin. Even if it was possible to overlook her features, which it wasn't, she had a natural elegance.

Tall and lanky, she wore her clothes well. Her beauty and manner were timeless. His breath hitched, and he couldn't prevent himself from taking her in. Despite her thin frame she was amply endowed.

Max swallowed. He remembered that dress from Friday night. The cleavage and what it hinted at.

Forcing his gaze away from her, he stood, poised and ready. "Okay, it isn't heavy but a little bulky. I'll need your help, um..."

"Sophie," she rescued him and held out her hand to exchange greetings. "I overheard your name is Maximilian. That's formal, isn't it?" When she smiled it reached her eyes and make them sparkle. Friendly. Trusting. Max had a sense she wasn't all that she seemed. What a mess. He hated asking her for help, owing her, getting someone else involved in his family drama, but he really needed to get paid.

"Max," he said more bluntly than he intended. He was befuddled. Sophie moved closer to him and overwhelmed his senses. He wanted to reach out and stroke her lovely skin that he knew was oh-so-soft to the touch.

Weird. Of course, his mind turned to stunning artistic figures from history, works of Botticelli or Klimt, all gold and irresistible. Sophie could be one of them. Max had a powerful urge to paint her, and that wasn't his usual medium. He preferred tactile clays and timbers and objects that could be manipulated to his will.

Enough. He was losing his mind.

Sophie moved over to the object and grasped it from underneath.

He rushed over. "Careful."

"Jeez. You said it wasn't heavy," she said and burst into giggles. Promptly, she placed it down. "I'm not sure I can do this."

"Oh, c'mon. You're the only one here. I carried it in alone. It's not hard. I'll take the bulk of the weight." He lifted the bottom. Sophie followed and they took baby steps towards her car.

"What is this anyway?"

"It's a sculpture."

"A sculpture? As in art? I'd really love to take a look."

Max ignored the statement. Clearly, she was being polite. There was no way he was unwrapping it before delivery.

Concentrating, they moved along the path towards the fence. Sophie fumbled over her own feet and the package slipped.

"Watch it," he yelled as he pushed his knees forward to balance his body weight around it. He bumped into her and threw her off balance. Sophie teetered than veered into the garden bed.

"You almost dropped it," he snapped and pulled the piece out of her grasp. The car was at the kerb and he slowly manoeuvred the package by himself the remainder of the way.

Chapter Seven

"Hey, where's your Porsche?"

"My Porsche?" Sophie chuckled. "I didn't bring that car today. Today is a Beamer day."

Okay, a Porsche and a BMW. Definitely one of *that crowd.*

They travelled in silence, except when Max provided directions. All the while it was on the tip of his tongue to disclose that Mrs Cartwright was his mother, but he thought he better not. Sophie would have an opinion of him based on his parents' wealth, and while he shouldn't care what some random chick who ran in his family's circle thought of him, he did. She did something to him. Yeah, the physical was obvious, but there was something more. He couldn't put his finger on it, but it bothered him as much as it intrigued him.

He mentally debated the issue until they arrived at Diane's PR agency.

Before Sophie could offer assistance, he jumped out of the car. "I don't need any help." In the event he had to plead for payment, he didn't want an audience. The embarrassment would be too great.

***

Sophie took the opportunity to check her work emails on her phone as she sat in the car waiting for the petulant, gorgeous, infuriating man. Nothing urgent from work. Everything would have to wait until she returned from Morocco anyway.

Minutes later she spied Max walking out of the agency. He dropped into the passenger seat, and said, "I owe you a drink for your help. There's a bar not far from here, my shout."

Sophie stared, tongue-tied. Was this the same guy who had bitten her head off repeatedly? Obviously, he was happy he'd made his delivery. Perhaps he was stressed earlier. Whatever.

She checked the time. Not quite three. Gaby was at home, and Sophie wouldn't be long.

Before she changed her mind, she blurted, "Okay."

Max gave her directions and she drove quickly. Now she was rethinking her yes. Spontaneity wasn't her thing. She planned, plotted, sometimes plodded, and looked at all the angles before putting her toe in the water. Diving in was not in Sophie's character. She should be going home, getting ready for her work trip, spending time with Gaby and preparing them for week ahead.

Sophie always did the right thing. Having been her sister's carer since Gaby was twelve meant Sophie had missed a lot of fun. Parties, nights out drinking with the girls, socialising with the opposite sex, and generally being a young woman enjoying life. It had passed her by. She'd never been drunk. Sometimes she acted like she was forty. Oh, hell. She'd embrace this moment and enjoy being with moody Max who was, at least, easy on the eyes.

Seated at a cosy corner table in the upscale bar, Sophie relaxed. This seemed to be the kind of place she'd chose to go. Not seedy and full of people who looked like they'd knife you in the alley.

After their drinks arrived, she sipped her bubbles and he enjoyed a cold beer. The place was quiet with few customers on a Monday afternoon, and surprisingly, Max made her feel comfortable. It helped that he was gorgeous. Would it be weird if she pretended they were on a date?

Their knees touched under the small table. Now being so close, she caught his essence, which was unusual. She inhaled deeply to identify it, and her nose tingled. Not body odour, and it wasn't offensive, but rather like her dad's back shed all those years ago where he'd tinker and fix things. Glue? Perhaps, and a bit like cleaning products: ammonia or turps maybe. Not unpleasant, but it didn't make her want to rip his clothes off and dip her face in it, which was a good thing. Max was a complication she couldn't afford on any level.

Now that she was paying closer attention, his clothes were too loose and were dulled by wear. Was that a stain on his jeans that looked like a splatter of paint? His shirt was crumpled as if he'd slept in it, and she had to say, he looked like a bit of a grub.

The silence dragged and they both took another sip of their drinks.

"Do you come here often?" Max said and they both broke out into laughter, easing the tension. "I'm so sorry. That was lame." He knocked his palm against his forehead. "I was trying to make conversation."

Was he nervous? Sophie loved that he seemed vulnerable, especially since he'd been less than friendly until now. He acted relaxed, but his leg shook under the table. "I don't go out that much," she said.

"Me neither," he replied. 'Is it 'cause you're always working?'

Sophie shook her head and her hair swung around her shoulders. "I work full time and attend lots of events after hours where I have to be social. Usually I'm so tired, all I want to do is go home and get off my feet."

He nodded in understanding. "What's a personal stylist? Do you style people?" he joked.

"Basically, yes. Lilly Malone is a luxury fashion label. I help clients chose clothes that suit them along with accessories, and any other products we sell. It is about making women feel good."

"Women need help from another woman to pick out their clothes?" He sounded incredulous.

"It's a thing. But in fairness, it's way more than that. It's a holistic service," she said knowing it sounded pretentious. She drained the rest of her drink to avoid saying more.

She didn't want to talk about her. Often, she screamed with frustration of surrounding herself with shallow, rich, spoilt people, but then she knew she sounded ungrateful and like a brat. Her job paid the bills, and that was all that mattered. Was it her passion? No. The last thing she wanted to bang on about today was the reality of being trapped in a job, especially when she was beginning to enjoy herself.

A guy thwacked Max's back, which caused his beer to spill over the edge of its glass.

"Mate," the guy bellowed.

Max turned his head. "Luke, how are you? Feeling better?"

"Yeah. Thanks for covering for me the other night, I owe you one. A drink?"

"Luke, this is Sophie. Sophie this is one of my best mates, Luke."

"Nice to meet you, Sophie. Can I get you another glass of bubbles?"

"I can't stay long," Sophie responded, looking at Max. "I have to get home to pack for Morocco, I'm flying out tonight."

Max spluttered his mouthful of beer, and the liquid sprayed across the tabletop.

Sophie sat back in her chair.

Oh, bugger.

She wanted gobble the words back up. Damn it. Max didn't say anything, but tried to mop up the mess with their little cocktail napkins. Luke's brows rose on his forehead.

Idiot, Sophie. Sometimes she sounded like the people she worked for.

She smiled. Not knowing how to recover the situation, she said to Luke, "I'd love another one please." He responded by heading to the bar. Max rose to go with him, surely running away from her.

This was what came from not having a normal social life. She didn't know how to act and what to say.

They came back a few minutes later, and Sophie gulped down the contents of flute placed in front of her .Luke politely kept her in the conversation with meaningless small talk, but Max didn't say another word to her. The rude prick had returned.

After the last sip she rose, and slid her bag over her shoulder. "Thanks for the drinks. Nice to meet you, Luke. Sorry, I have to go." She half ran out of the bar.

Max let her leave without a word.

Chapter Eight

Sophie lugged her Lilly Malone suitcase up the stairwell of her apartment complex. The bang of the metal wheels against the steps echoed around her. Her heart beat a little faster, not from the exertion, but at the prospect of seeing Gaby. Five days wasn't long, but she'd missed her sister something awful.

Her arm glowed bronzed against the silver balustrade. She hadn't spent time sunbaking in the glorious Moroccan heat, but Mrs Helibronn never did anything the easy way. They'd had many consultations poolside while her client sipped exotic cocktails and applied oil to her already burned skin.

Mrs Helibronn had been holidaying with her husband, but Sophie hadn't seen him once. She did, however, spot many a local man happy to apply sunscreen on Mrs Helibronn. As usual, the trip had been an experience, and she had many stories to share with Gaby. But most importantly, her luggage was lighter on the return home, having sold most of it to the happy client who now sat somewhere in Africa with her swanky new wardrobe.

Reaching the second level, Sophie placed her suitcase down to catch her breath. The aging complex hadn't been refurbished and didn't have a lift. It kept her fit, and more importantly, the rent was low.

Mrs Miller descended the stairs from level three. "Hello, dear. I thought I heard you. I'm so glad you're home."

Sophie's pulse accelerated at the words and her stance went rigid. She placed her hands on her hips to keep her balance. "Hello, Mrs Miller. What's wrong?" Her words were a whisper.

"Gaby felt unwell so we called an ambulance and went to the hospital."

Sophie's chest constricted so tight she couldn't breath and she doubled over at the waist.

Mrs Miller tottered over with the assistance of her walking stick and placed a warm hand to her back. "It happened late yesterday, and she's been overnight at the hospital."

Sophie nodded. "Thank you so much for caring for her."

Her face must've shown her fear. Mrs Miller patted her on the back like a doting grandma. "She'll be fine, dear. The doctor said so."

Yes, she would be, but Sophie should've been here. She should've been the one to take Gaby to the hospital, sit with her to make sure she wasn't afraid. Hold her hand. This job kept them alive, but it also destroyed Sophie.

Opening her apartment door, she dumped her suitcase, turned, and rushed back out.

***

"How did your sugar levels get so low?"

Gaby and Sophie lazed around at home the following morning eating smashed avo on whole-wheat toast with apple juice from the trendy new breakfast place downstairs. A rare treat.

"It was sports day on Thursday, and it had been super hot. We'd been busy throughout the day. I'd run a few races, and then Mrs Watson asked me to help with the younger kids. You know how it goes. I was distracted and didn't eat or drink enough water, and I was running around in the heat. My insulin doses weren't quite right. It actually wasn't a big deal, but later that night my levels were really low."

"How were you feeling at that point?"

"Not great. Shaking and sweating."

Sophie gasped. This wasn't good news, but they'd had this struggle for years and understood how to battle it.

"Okay, I agree that isn't great. What did you do then?"

"I knew what to do but I was so tired, and I couldn't find any jelly beans, so I had a few teaspoons of honey…"

Doing her best mother imitation, Sophie gave her a disapproving look.

"I know, right, but I was exhausted, and it isn't Mrs Miller's job to feed me. To cut a long story short, my levels would usually pick up after fifteen minutes or so, as they always have in the past. Not this time. I made myself a piece of toast but that didn't seem to help either. I talked it over with Mrs Miller who panicked. She made me panic. Together we agreed it was best to make the trip to the hospital."

"I'm so sorry I wasn't here. I'm pretty sure I could have got those levels back to normal."

Gaby's smile lit up the room. Even through all the adversity, this kid remained positive.

"You know what? It was fine, and the hospital got it under control quickly. When they realised Mrs Miller wasn't my mother or grandmother, they refused to release me into the care of a seventy-year-old."

"Poor, Mrs Miller. She certainly had a fright." Sophie prayed this hiccup wouldn't mean Mrs Miller be unwilling to help again. What would Sophie do then? "We'll have to take her a lasagne to say thank you."

"Everything is fine. I could have easily had an episode if you'd been here."

Sophie said nothing and leaned over to kiss Gaby's forehead. How did this kid get so smart? Sophie's insides were melting. They always did when it came to Gaby. Since caring for her sister, Sophie well and truly understood the unconditional love parents had for their children and the sacrifices they were prepared to make.

"I'm staying in this weekend and resting," Gaby said. "I'll do some more homework later if I can manage. I don't want to get behind. That doesn't mean you have to hang here. Why don't you go out and have some fun?"

Fun. What was that? It had become an abstract concept. That is, until she'd spent that afternoon with Max. Then she'd opened her big mouth and sounded like a privileged brat, and he'd clammed up.

Bugger him. He didn't know anything about her. He sure was quick to judge. Even though he'd reverted to prick, it hadn't kept him out of her thoughts. It didn't help that he was the first male interaction she'd had in forever. She touched her knee where it had connected with his under the table. *Stop being ridiculous.* That knee had been washed a dozen times since then. His touch wasn't easy to forget, though, or maybe it was those dreamy, dark, and brooding looks. Her fingers still longed to touch his beard.

Gaby rose to go and lie down.

"Yeah, if you're sure, I might go out for a bit. I'll be back to make dinner, and I'll have my phone on me, you can ring anytime."

"Sure," her sister said, "that sounds great, enjoy yourself."

Sophie felt a spark of excitement ignite inside her. A couple of hours to herself. Morocco had been busy, busy, busy. Downtime happened only in between Mrs Helibronn's never-ending requests, and then Sophie usually slept or caught up on paperwork.

But now, Sophie knew exactly where to go, and she couldn't wait.

Chapter Nine

The cool museum welcomed Sophie as she entered through double glass spring-back doors. They suctioned shut after her and she moved out of the passageway and paused. Silence, pure and real surrounded her as calm descended like a cloak. She loved the unspoken code required for entry: talk in hushed voices. Viewing art required peace and reflection. She breathed in possibility and revelled in the serene atmosphere.

It had been too long.

Visitors milled around the entrance, stopping to admire books in the shop before heading into the spacious galleries containing the latest pieces.

Only recently, a new exhibition had opened featuring some of the greatest impressionist works from the *Musee D'Orsay* in France. Impressionism was her absolute favourite. The muted and subtle colours and undeniable beauty of the works of Monet and Pissarro made her stomach flip. She couldn't wait.

The Impressionist exhibit was at the rear of the museum, and no hardship, she had to wander through other rooms first. Sophie followed a crowd off to the left that entered a gallery space. Immediately she realised it was the private gallery where local Brisbane residents sold their work.

The opening had created quite a buzz a few years ago. Before then, artists only had the choice to sell their work at small, suburban and privately-owned galleries, often with hefty commissions. Sophie hadn't been in here since the museum had opened the shop.

The room had a different vibe from the museum galleries. While the money still smelled old and heavy, the work was diverse and modern.

A stunning piece stood out and she gravitated towards it. Her brain couldn't take in the painting in one glance. The work took up most of the wall. Goose bumps nubbed her skin as she gazed at the deep blue landscape of icicles and white-water tips, and the wildlife that only survived in the freezing conditions. She could almost feel the cold.

Sophie stared, drawn into its depths. Mrs Keyes, another of her VIP clients—weren't they all—had been hunting for a breathtaking landscape painting as a surprise for her husband's birthday. Price wasn't a concern. Sophie quickly scanned the painting for a sold sticker and didn't spot one.

Whipping out her phone, she telephoned her client. After sneaking an image via her mobile and a hushed and quick telephone call, Sophie tilted her chin in the direction of a staff member to gain his attention.

She waited, and a figure appeared beside her, standing too close, his presence objectionable. Annoyed at her personal space being invaded, she turned to face the culprit. Max.

Her heart accelerated and beat like a drum in her chest while a strange thrill bounced into the pit of her stomach. No man had ever had this physiological effect on her. Only Max. It was unsettling, and a damn nuisance.

"Hello. What a surprise seeing you here," she greeted him with a tight smile. She wondered if he be friendly and gentle Max or the rude and obnoxious version. Why she cared was beyond her comprehension.

Before Max could utter 'hello,' a staff member approached. "Ms Williams?"

Sophie nodded and uttered, an unintelligible, "Mmhmm," to the gentleman who addressed her. She was all too aware of Max and his gaze boring into her. She couldn't mess this up. Mrs Keyes counted on her.

"You spoke to us about purchasing this outstanding painting and we can confirm that this one is still available for sale. Would you like to proceed?"

"Yes, thank you so much. I would like to purchase it. It's truly beautiful. What information do you need from me?"

The gentleman held a clipboard with sheets of paper attached and a pen poised in his hand. He shuffled them trying to find something.

Despite willing herself not to, she glanced at the price tag at the lower bottom edge of the painting. $15,000 screamed out in bold, gold print. Max followed her stare. His body stiffened. She really wanted to turn away, turn her back on him, but like a child being told to keep her eyes shut, she couldn't ignore him.

Damn, he was distracting. His expression was stiff and pulled so tight his features appeared to have turned to stone. But they weren't, because then he whistled. He seemed to be deliberately belligerent. Why couldn't he have turned up five minutes later?

Sophie swivelled fast and narrowed her eyes at him and stared open-mouthed hoping to convey her irritation before turning back to provide the staff member with the required information.

Max went quiet and it became easier to ignore him.

Needing to provide payment, she reached for her mobile phone and rang Mrs Keyes. As the dial tone pealed, she looked for Max, but he was gone. Sophie turned a circle and spotted him three metres away, admiring another piece. Possibly sensing her glare, his gaze shifted and briefly locked with hers. He stopped staring first.

At the conclusion of the sale, her client squealed and uttered promises she'd never keep, and Sophie had to hold the phone away from her ear.

She took a deep breath and glanced around to find Max. He was still here. One part of her hoped he'd disappeared while the other was a little intrigued.

"Who are you, really?" he muttered as she'd arrived by his side. Max's lips were pinched as he poked at her, and he didn't allow her time to respond. "No one I know who has a normal job can waltz into the private gallery and purchase a $15,000 painting, let alone a $3,000 one." While he continued his interrogation, his voice got louder. "You tell me you're a lowly personal stylist," he spat the words, "but that doesn't seem likely. Are you famous? Rich? Is your family wealthy? Are you a drug dealer?" He gesticulated wildly, and looked like a clown.

Sophie rolled her eyes. Patrons stared. She placed her hand on one of his flailing arms and held it firm. His skin was warm to the touch. "Are you finished?"

Max's jaw locked and he glared at her.

"People are staring, and frankly, you're being ridiculous and don't know what you are talking about. I don't need to defend myself to you." Sophie took a step back to regain the control she was losing. She held her shaking hands to prevent herself from poking him in the chest.

Contrition spread across his features, and he shook his head. "I'm sorry." He grasped her elbow and pulled her along. They walked until he paused in front of a sculpture.

"Do you like this piece?" he asked, his voice soft as his eyes searched her face.

"What?" Was this guy for real? He ran hot and cold like a broken faucet. Serious and serene, he stood next to her as if he hadn't been making a scene two minutes ago.

Sophie couldn't figure him out. She should walk away. He required too much effort and was trouble. She wasn't going anywhere. Her feet seemed locked to the spot.

It wasn't his seductive good looks, though they helped. It was the mischievous glint that sparkled in his eye, and the way they bored into her as if trying to access her innermost soul. He was a complex enigma, and she was unfortunately drawn to him. Ripples of fear and exhilaration ran through her at the same time, giving her a headache.

Max stared at the piece sitting atop a pedestal column. Sophie needed to somehow disrupt the electricity between them. An invisible force kept pulling her to him, like they were connected.

She broke free and walked a circle around the sculpture. Made of a textured orange clay, the work was of a seated headless woman with a torso of fluid and smooth curves. A swollen breast drooped on a round stomach while long, slim legs were crossed. So simple and provocative, the piece caused her to suck in her breath.

"It's beautiful."

Max beamed.

Chapter Ten

She liked the sculpture, and thought it was beautiful.

"Do you like it?" she asked.

"You said you're interested in art, right?"

"I am. I don't always understand it, but something about the timeless grandeur captured in each piece, whether it's a drawing or painting, or a sculpture," Sophie gestured toward the one they admired, "is special."

"What do you like about this one?" he asked.

"I like that it doesn't have a face to distract us with notions of beauty usually associated with looks. Without it, we can focus on her lines and shape."

Max nodded.

"I want to touch her, feel her curves." Sophie lifted her fingers toward it.

Max grasped them and lowered them by his side and Sophie laughed. "I wasn't really going to touch it." A light musical titter washed over him, tantalising his senses. He hadn't heard her laugh much and he liked it.

"I think you understand more than you think."

Still holding her fingers in the tips of his, Max moved closer to find a sale sticker. No red dot. His shoulders slumped slightly.

"Hang on," Sophie said and looked between him and the sculpture and back again. Dropping his fingers, she stuck her head close to the piece. "This is for sale, too."

He nodded.

Sophie's head tilted in contemplation and her brow creased. He imagined the connections swirling in her mind trying to gain traction as she gazed off into the distance. He wouldn't say it.

"Is this yours?" she finally asked.

"Yeah. I'm an artist, well. Sculptor mainly. I prefer creating things with my hands, but I can paint and draw."

"Oh, Max, this is beautiful. You're so talented." Her lips curved upwards into a smile that illuminated her face and highlighted her sparkling eyes. Her reaction convinced him she meant what she said. His chest puffed out.

"The one you delivered the other day to Mrs Cartwright's, was that one of your pieces, too?"

"Yeah. I don't receive many commissions, but Diane from the PR Agency specifically asked for a piece to display in their office space."

Max continued to stare at his art, fixated on the price. It was impossible not to dream of how he'd spend those four figures. Adrenalin surged through him and he fought the urge to run, run fast and hard, and as far away as possible. Instead, he clenched his fists. God, he needed that money.

As if she could read his mind, Sophie said, "I'm sure someone will buy it soon."

Max shrugged.

Sophie jumped on the spot. "Oh, you know what? I know someone who'd buy this…"

Max's hackles got up. "What, you? A sympathy buy? No, thank you." He hated the hard edge that had returned to his voice. He walked away. Annoyed, he needed to get a grip on his emotions, and he would, but he had to calm down first.

She followed him into the open area of the museum and they mixed in with the swarm of people heading towards the Impressionist exhibit. He joined the queue for tickets and felt Sophie next to him.

They purchased their tickets in silence and moved their way into the gallery.

He paused in front of a Monet. Sophie ogled it and she positioned herself to eye it closely. This girl was something else.

"I love this piece. I love beautiful things," she said without diverting her eyes. Finishing her appraisal, she moved close to him and folded her arms across her chest. "You owe me an apology."

"For what?" He knew he was being childish, but he couldn't seem to stop himself.

"You don't know anything about me yet you accuse me of being something I'm not. I've told you what I do for a living. Why are you so upset that I was buying a painting for one of my clients?"

"Your client?" He paused, thinking. "Purchasing art is part of your job?" The moment he said the words, a sinking feeling arose that perhaps he wasn't making the right connections.

"Yes, a client. If you'd asked, or let me explain, I'd have told you. Do I look like I can afford a $15,000 painting?"

Bugger, he'd reacted without thinking. Around her he was all emotions and no brain. Max regarded her, watching as feigned innocence spread across her features. He couldn't help it, he smiled at her theatrics.

His behaviour, on the other hand, wasn't funny. "Okay. You're right. I owe you an apology. I'm sorry, I really am. I jumped to conclusions."

She nodded her acceptance, and they continued to saunter amongst the greats of the past. Max spied the cafe. "Let me make it up to you. Can I buy you a coffee?"

Sophie checked her watch—she did that a lot—and then agreed.

Once they were seated with steaming flat whites in front of them on the open deck of the museum snack bar, Max said, "You have a strange job."

She considered him. "I guess I do."

"I'm sorry I made assumptions. I can be impulsive. So I understand, is purchasing other items, that's not clothes or jewellery, part of your job description when you are dressing a client for your clothing label?"

"I guess it sounds weird. My job is to dress and assist clients with Lilly Malone products. They get access to new season designs before anyone else, exclusive offers, and other goodies. After spending so much time with my clients, I've gotten to know these women well and I aim to please them as part of my holistic service. One of my clients was searching for a special gift for her husband's fiftieth birthday. I thought of her immediately when I saw the painting. It is beautiful, right? Did you see it?"

Max nodded, then took a sip of coffee. "Yeah, spectacular."

"Right, so I was helping her out."

"I'm assuming all of your clients are wealthy?"

"Most of them. I mean, who has a personal shopper doing their bidding when they can go into an atelier on their own? It's beyond extraordinary, it's indulgent."

He enjoyed listening to her. Sophie continued on, talking animatedly about her love of art. Occasionally she placed her hand over his on the table. It seemed an unconscious movement and as her stories progressed, she'd remove it. He loved that she was comfortable with him. As she spoke, he got lost in her voice, her dark eyes, the gestures, and he found himself leaning in closer, completely engrossed, his head supported by his hand.

Man, it was nice to be thinking of other things and not absorbed in his constant fear of where his next dollar would come from.

Sophie checked the time and jumped up. They'd been talking for well over an hour.

"What's wrong?"

"The museum closes in forty-five minutes and we haven't seen the rest of the Impressionists. I'm not sure when I'll get back again. Can we keep looking?"

He loved that too. She expected him to finish the exhibit with her. "Sure. Let's go." He was disappointed though. He could've listened to her for hours.

Max's interest wasn't on the art. His focus was on Sophie. She regarded each painting intensely, examined the detail and commented on what she liked and didn't. Occasionally, she asked him a question, and she had to repeat it, so deep into being with her, he was in a bit of a daze.

Nearing the exit, he asked, "Can I duck back into the private gallery for a second?" Max raced away before she could answer.

With low expectations, he approached his sculpture and scanned for the elusive red dot.

Sophie came up behind him. He spotted it and turned and embraced her, chuffing with glee.

"It's sold, Sophie. I can't believe it." The swell of her breasts squeezed against his chest and he held tighter. The citrus scent of her hair tickled his nose as it brushed against him.

She hugged him back. "I'm so excited for you."

"We need to celebrate. Let's have dinner tonight."

She dropped her smile. "Oh, I'm sorry, but I can't. I have to get home." She checked the time again and took two steps toward the exit.

He deflated. "Wait," he grasped her arm. "Please."

Her gaze swept his, and he watched a battle wage behind her eyes. Her shoulders hunched. Moments passed.

"Do you want to come to my place? I can't go out tonight, but I'll make you dinner." Sophie licked her lips. All the blood in his body drained to his groin.

Without waiting for his response, she reached for his hand, laced her fingers with his, and they left the museum.

Chapter Eleven

"Hello. I'm home," Sophie sung out as she pushed open the front door. She'd never called out her arrival before—who else would it be—but she'd never brought a man home before either.

Unable to punch out a text message of warning to her sister, Sophie hoped calling out would get Gaby out into the hallway. It worked. Her sister wandered out of her bedroom. She was in her comfy clothes: grey track pants and a loose t-shirt. Her long auburn hair was pulled into a messy bun. A pencil jutted out from behind her right ear. She was probably doing homework.

Sophie winged it. She was unprepared for Max's and her sister's reactions, but acted like this happened every day. Sophie moved through the living room to the kitchen and dumped the grocery bags on the counter. She and Max had made a quick stop to pick up supplies. He followed her into the kitchen with the heavier bags. She turned to look at Gaby, whose eyes were wide, and a broad smile showed off all her straight, white teeth.

"Gaby, this is Max. Max, this is my sister Gaby."

Completely unfazed— she had no idea why she thought differently—Max stepped forward and held out his hand for Gaby to shake. She took it pumped vigorously while she continued to grin.

"Wow. You must be special. This is the first time Sophie has brought someone home. How did you two meet?" Gaby leaned against the counter looking smug. Sophie, who'd been putting things away, turned from the fridge, her back to Max, and gave Gaby a warning stare.

Gaby laughed.

"Really? I am special then. We met up at the museum today, but we've run into each other before at work events," he replied.

"I'm guessing you aren't a client who requires a stylist to assist them with filling their wardrobe with an excessive amount of clothes costing an exorbitant amount of money."

Max swept his body with his hands to indicate his attire. "Clearly you can work that out."

Sophie considered his outfit. He looked damn fine. His clothes clung to his body most appealingly. There was nothing wrong with his casual ensemble. A slave to fashion wouldn't embrace non-designer jeans and an average deep orange polo, but Max wore it well. The shirt's colour suited his dark features. Unlike last time, today he was tidy. Suddenly, the penny dropped. His paint-splattered gear must've been his work clothes.

"There's nothing wrong with what you're wearing," Sophie stated. Max smiled in return.

"That's a compliment coming from Sophie. Most days she's showing off fancy frills, flamboyant colours, and low necklines," Gaby said.

Sophie protested, "I need to represent the brand and have to dress up—"

"I'm kidding, Soph." Gaby turned to Max. "Actually, she's much more comfortable in her vintage attire, but that won't sell the couture clothes."

Changing the subject, Sophie said, "It's still early. Should we have a drink and some nibbles and sit on the balcony for a while? Then I can make dinner."

"Sounds great," Max said. "How can I help?"

Sophie passed him the bottle of white wine and two glasses. His thick, calloused fingers circled hers. One finger caressed her pinkie as their gazes connected. Sophie's body got warm, and a strange thrill rippled through her stomach. Heat seemed to radiate off him, and his eyes flashed at the contact.

Sophie desperately wanted to kiss those full lips and have them against her neck, where they'd travel... She had to stop this. She extracted her hand and left him to pour as she made up platters of cheeses and dips.

"Gaby, join us."

"Yep, okay. This looks so good. I have to have some salami and cheese. It's been ages since we've eaten this. A quick bite, and then I'll study until dinner."

"Do you feel all right?"

Gaby nodded.

They sat at their circular glass table on the tiny deck. Max asked Gaby, "Have you been unwell?"

"Nothing out of the ordinary. I have Type One diabetes and it's an effort to keep my sugar levels right. During the week Sophie was in Morocco I was busy at school and it was super-hot, and I wasn't paying as close attention to keeping hydrated and eating as I should have. I had to go to hospital, and now I need to rest, but I have to study, which isn't taxing." Gaby smiled.

Sophie swelled with pride at her sister's spirit. Even after all she'd faced in her short life, she was still so upbeat. Sophie had a lot to learn from her little sister.

"That's why I couldn't go out tonight," Sophie said. "I need to be here with Gaby, at least for the next couple of days."

"You could've gone out, Soph. I would've been okay," Gaby protested.

Sophie shook her head. "I was away all week. I need to be here." As she took a sip of wine, Sophie was aware of Max watching the exchange.

"Are your parents here?" he asked.

Sophie and Gaby looked at each other. "Our parents died five years ago in a car accident. They were hit by a drunk driver. I've taken care of Gaby on my own," Sophie said, steadying herself for his reaction.

"I'm so sorry." He looked at them, his expression tight. "That must've been tough. You're amazing, Sophie. What a responsibility." He spoke with a sincerity and genuineness that was rare. Sophie spent most of her time with the elite and privileged to whom honesty and courtesy wasn't important.

"Sophie's always been there for me. She's worked to keep us clothed and fed."

Gaby drained the remainder of her wine.

"What year are you in, Gaby?"

"Twelve. It's a big year and I need to make sure I don't get sick too often. I can't afford to miss classes. It's too hard to catch up."

"What subjects are you studying?"

"Well," Gaby sat back with a slice of Camembert cheese and cracker, "I'm doing all the sciences. I'm thinking maybe veterinary studies or perhaps laboratory work or something similar. I'm not sure yet."

"I can't help her with her homework. I am the least science-oriented person I know," Sophie said.

"I guess there isn't much use for pattern matching or accessorising with that," Max smiled.

Was he being cheeky or belittling?

"No. Hasn't Sophie told you? Her passion is art. I think she'd be great as a gallery curator or manager, or maybe an art historian."

"You didn't tell me that," Max said.

"Well, ah, today is the first day we've had a proper conversation."

He laughed. "True. But I didn't realise when you said you loved art that's what you meant."

Gaby rose. "On that note, Sophie won't stop talking about now that she's started. I'm off to read my chemistry, which will be much more interesting than Monet," Gaby stated.

"You know, Max is an artist," Sophie yelled after her.

Gaby stopped at the balcony sliding door and regarded them, turning serious. "Wow. You guys are a perfect match," she said with a sly smile before she waltzed off.

With little view to enjoy off their pathetic tiled deck, they watched a blazing sunset as the cool evening breeze rushed in.

Sophie relaxed and remembered how it felt to be young and as if nothing in the world mattered. That summed up her time with Max. He amused her with his turn of phrase and light mocking. He made her feel good, and she couldn't remember the last person who did that.

She wished she could capture this vibrancy and bottle it up for the times she struggled to pretend her day was bright. For the mornings when she didn't bounce out of bed.

For so long, her and Gaby's future had been uncertain. Each day had been a struggle until her job had saved them. Given them a future and money.

The immature, selfish part of her part longed to be like Max and do what she loved most. Her soul was destroyed a little each day as she pretended that the whims of the rich and bored mattered. In her room alone at night, she cried for lost dreams.

Max helped her feel vibrant and forget the responsibilities she bore. The ever-present question of *why did their parents have to die* didn't hang like a shroud on her skin when she was with Max.

He placed his hand on her bare knee. Her skin sizzled at his touch and all the heat in her body pooled below her waist. She felt her face flush.

She wanted to jump onto his lap to embrace him and kiss him. She longed to feel his lips against hers and run her fingers through his hair.

"You seem lost in thought."

"I don't often stop and enjoy a glass of wine or a chat. I'm enjoying it." Other comments sat on her tongue but she held them in, frightened to utter them.

"Me too. Thanks for inviting me over. I didn't realise you cared for your sister. It's been great meeting her and learning more about you. You're not what I thought."

"You were quick to judge me."

Max nodded and chuckled lightly. "I'm sorry. It's impossible not to."

Sophie smiled tightly not sure where this was heading.

"First time I met you, you're jumping out of a Porsche and rammed your door into my car." He held up his hand to stop Sophie from interrupting. "And then, you're inside dressed to the nines as a guest at the party, and I'm there as the hired help serving drinks to the rich and famous. So, yeah, I think it was a fair assumption."

"Okay, maybe, but it took you a while to thaw."

"Let's say I haven't always had fulfilling relationships with people who have money. Excessive money changes people." His gaze turned toward the setting sun.

"Totally agree. I see it every day."

They sat silently for a moment. "If we're ever going to eat, I'd best start cooking." Sophie stood and collected the empty plates and her drained glass. The bottle of wine was empty.

"I'll help," Max said and together they walked inside.

Chapter Twelve

"Can I put on some tunes?"

Sophie agreed and Max placed his phone on the kitchen island so they could hear it.

Being in the kitchen with Sophie was fun. He hummed the words to the songs and found opportunities to stand behind her as she stirred the risotto. Her back rose and fell with her breaths. The proximity forced him to move back a step, any closer and Sophie might detect exactly how he felt about being this close to her.

Instead, he grabbed her and forced her to dance around the kitchen.

She giggled, and in response he twirled her and then did a deep dip before straightening, Sophie laughing in his arms.

He became sillier and she said, "You're not moody Max today. I like it." Her eyes shone bright and he knew she meant it as a tease.

He stopped his crazy dancing. "You know how you feel when you're a personal stylist to a wealthy and entitled woman who is making demands that you simply can't fulfil?"

"Yep. Worthless, futile, and dissatisfied."

He nodded. "That's how I feel when I'm forced to accept those hospitality jobs because I can't pay my rent." He pulled her in for a tango across the small kitchen space. "But not today. Today I've been paid."

The smile on her face was so wide her cheeks must have ached. He tried to focus on its dazzle and not the curve of her breast pinned against his chest. The music hit its crescendo and he upped his pace and swung her into another dip. He peered at her expectant one. They were so close he felt her shallow breathing and the quick lick of her lips.

Too much temptation.

He held her securely at the waist, leaned down, and kissed her.

Her lips were soft and she groaned when their mouths touched. It took all his effort not to pin her against the wall to feel those glorious curves. Instead, he raised her up until she faced him, and he didn't let her slip from his grasp. Searching her eyes, he sought her consent.

Sophie's pupils darkened and spelled desire.

Max inhaled deeply and placed one hand behind her head, running it through her loose hair before angling it to his needy mouth.

She didn't resist.

Their lips met, and he stroked her mouth in a series of feather-light touches, nipping at her. His will slipped away each time he tasted her, his passion building and he felt like he'd explode.

His pants tightened and he pushed himself against her, no longer afraid of her feeling his desire. His tongue found hers, and an electric current surged through his chest.

She responded to his need, and the kiss deepened, their mouths and tongues exploring. He placed his hands behind her head as she gripped his t-shirt. With one hand, she stroked his beard, gently at first and then harder until she held his chin in her grip.

Breathless, she pulled away first.

With wide eyes, her lips parted, and he saw her pink tongue dart out to lick her lips. The remembered taste made him want to thrust his tongue into her mouth again.

He held her close and felt her hard nipples through her shirt. Her fingers caressed his chin hair and slid along his cheek. He moved his hand from behind her head toward her breast. He cupped it and moulded the soft flesh in his hand. Behind them a bubbling sound became louder.

"Oh, shit, the risotto." Sophie dropped her hand from his face and turned to the stovetop. Max's hand was suddenly empty and cold.

Frantically, she stirred the stuck mixture from the base of the pan. He moved behind her and wrapped his arms around her middle. Her heart raced spurring him on. In a swift movement, he pushed her hair off her neck and peppered it with kisses. Her neck bent in response and she released another moan.

"I think it's ready," she whispered.

Whispering back, he said, "Well, we better eat then before our appetite is otherwise satisfied." He spun her around and landed one last kiss. He'd meant it to be fast and a reminder of what else would come, but she met his desire as if she couldn't have cared less if the dinner burned and they starved.

Their lips lingered, touching lightly and tantalising him as they brushed against each other with their hot breaths. Pulling apart, they panted as their foreheads touched.

"I'd best serve dinner. Gaby could walk in at any moment."

Lost for words, Max nodded.

***

Their desire simmered over dinner. Their legs touched under the table, and they exchanged mischievous grins. After Gaby took her last mouthful, she pushed her bowl aside and reached to the shelf for Trivial Pursuit. "Let's play a game."

Sophie and Max both groaned. "She only wants to play because she knows she'll absolutely blast us. I'm terrible at general knowledge but I guess, we'll blitz the arty ones," Sophie said.

Max shrugged. "I'm game if you are."

"Let's do it."

Gaby squealed with delight as she won round after round. Max and Sophie playfully high-fived when they scored a win, but underneath the table they couldn't stop touching each other. The wine they were downing aided in spurring them on.

Gaby raised her arms in victory and declared herself the smartest person in the house. Max and Sophie smiled.

He moved his chair back from the table and stood. "It's late, I should go." He stared at Sophie. "Gaby, it was great to meet you. And yeah, you're the brainiac." He ruffled her hair.

Gaby pushed his hand away and stood quickly to embrace him.

***

Sophie registered Max's surprise at Gaby's display of affection. He hugged her back. His long arms almost went double around her small frame. Sophie's heart jumped to her throat and she muffled a sob.

"See you soon, Max. Good night," Gaby called as she near skipped away.

Sophie stood. At the start of the day, she'd never have contemplated Max would be standing in her home and they'd have shared a passionate kiss. One she couldn't wait to duplicate. She'd not had many boyfriends and none worth remembering. Most of them were fumbled experiences of embarrassment in the bedroom and even worse, fake romantic sentiments.

She was confused and uncertain if she should invite him to stay.

Max carried the dirty bowls to the sink and tidied up quickly. Maybe he didn't want to stay. At that thought, she bit the inside of her cheek and held her body taut.

He approached and her stomach did a little flip before he pulled her into a tight embrace. She lost her breath he squeezed so hard. His lips were on hers and it was like they'd never stopped kissing. His taste was inviting and descendant, and after two kisses, familiar.

This time, his kiss was hard and demanding without any of the gentleness from before. His hand fondled her butt before roaming fast over her body as if desperate to feel every part of her. She gravitated to him with her hips poised for maximum contact. She wanted to be closer still, to give her body the thrill it desired. It came alive and responded, reaching for—

"Sophie," her sister yelled from inside her bedroom. "My sugar reading is really low."

Sophie jerked away. She wiped the back of her hand against her raw lips and felt the swelling. The bristle of his beard prickled her sensitive skin.

"I've got to go."

Max nodded. "I hope she's okay."

Sophie raced to Gaby hoping the same thing.

Chapter Thirteen

Another Friday and another Lilly Malone event. Shutting her eyes, Sophie savoured the cold drink as it fizzed down her throat. Her third champagne and finally the tightly wound coils in her back unravelled. If her life didn't slow down soon, she might become an alcoholic, and that was the last thing she needed.

Looking across the room she searched for Max who was filling in for Luke again. There was standing room only at the bar, and the queue crept across the dance floor.

Her head throbbed at her temples. Tonight was important: a VIP Lilly Malone exclusive release. A thank you to customers, but also a premium opportunity to seize on pre-release items or exclusives and discounted sales.

Sophie prayed that a pair of the previous released designer sneakers would appear like an apparition and save her skin. She'd yet to solve that problem, and it contributed to her aching head. She opened her bag and searched in its deep depths for paracetamol. Damnit, she'd run out. In place of the drugs, she rubbed her temples.

"Hello, Sophie," Ms Appleby said. A millionaire by the age of twenty-five, the same age as Sophie, who refused to focus on the obvious lack of similarity between them.

How different her life could've been if only she'd invented an organic skin care range using environmental ingredients and sourcing cheap labour in non-child slave countries. Sophie Williams could be an entrepreneur, but she hadn't invented anything. At least Ms Appleby made a difference, unlike many of the others in the room.

Stop it. You're doing the most important thing. Taking care of Gaby.

Sophie sighed. "Hello, Ms Appleby. You look stunning tonight."

Ms Appleby dazzled with a smile and patted the base of her perfect, blonde bob. "Thank you, darling. It's all because of you, of course. Anything here tonight you'd recommend?"

Sophie launched into what special items might be of interest. She'd learned early on that she had to tailor her responses to each client. In the beginning, young and naïve, she'd developed a spiel on each new item and repeated it verbatim. Of course, she realised too late, if her recommendations were accepted, it became difficult to fulfil numerous requests for the same item, or worse, inevitably her clients, who moved in similar social circles would commit social *faux paux* and attend an event in an identical outfit to their friend, or more catastrophic, their enemy. Sophie was smarter now and all of her advice was customised to whomever she spoke with. She knew her clients well.

Ms Appleby became engrossed in conversation about someone's ski trip to Verbier and Sophie took the opportunity to cross the room.

To Max. He was the only person she wanted to talk to. Standing alone at the end of the bar, he gulped down a glass of water during a brief lull of service.

"Hey," she said as she sidled up next to him.

"Hey, yourself," he said and offered her a bright smile. "You're looking gorgeous as usual."

"Why, thank you." Sophie flounced the base of her short dress. "I do particularly love this one. It's more my style, don't you think?" Sophie watched his gaze run from her head to her toes. The sleeveless red and white dress had a paisley print with two frills in the skirt. It was fun, practical, and pretty. Such an easy product to endorse. "This is a new release and already it's gaining lots of attention. Everyone is loving it. I've been stopped a million times tonight. Inez will be so pleased. I think they're going to release it in a few different colours. I've matched it with my own accessories, though, so I'm comfortable tonight."

Max listened to her, but his eyes diverted around the room. He was working.

"Problem is everyone wants to know about my earrings. It's a bit tricky to say these vintage emerald earrings are from my local second-hand store."

"Yeah. I think that's a secret best kept to yourself. Perhaps you can start to design some items for Lilly Malone," Max suggested.

Sophie punched him in his bicep. The muscle was hard. "I'm flattered you think I'm that talented. They pay designers big dollars to make extraordinary outfits. I'm not sure I fit in that category."

"How's Gaby?"

"She's okay. A head cold can cause a big fluctuation in her levels. She's not one hundred percent, but she's gone to a friend's house tonight because she's been at home all week and is going a bit nuts. I know and trust her friend's mum, so she'll be well looked after." Sophie gazed across the room. "She's having a bad run at the moment. It happens." She shrugged but her nonchalance did not in any way sum up her agonising week of worrying over Gaby and fitting in the demands of work.

Max nodded and touched her arm. It'd been a tough week. They'd arranged to meet a few times, but in the end had managed only a brief coffee, and even then Sophie'd been distracted and anxious. Similar to mothers she guessed. She felt she needed to be with Gaby whenever she wasn't at the office. Particularly when her sister felt unwell.

She'd neglected Max, and that worried her. Her week had exploded, and she simply hadn't had a spare minute except for when she was asleep. God it was exhausting. How could she contemplate adding more to her life? She didn't have time to devote to someone else. Hell, she didn't have time to look after herself. She needed to split herself three ways. But in the end, Max had seemed okay with it. Sophie ignored the shout in her head screaming his laidback attitude wouldn't last.

Thirsty people milled around the bar and Max got back to work. "Would you like a drink?" he asked before rushing behind the bar.

"Champagne, please." Before he accepted any new orders, he poured her a glass. "Have you had anything to eat?" His brow furrowed.

"Um, no, but I will now. I promise," she said and mock saluted him. He rushed away and a wave of emotion hit her.

She remembered his lips on hers and the feel of his body. Would she experience that again tonight? The thrill of anticipation had her floating away.

Announcements calling for donations to the evening's charity and for bids on the silent auction sounded over the room. Sophie paused at the table loaded with gifts.

One pamphlet depicted an ocean liner floating through crisp, light blue water at the edges of a tropical island flanked by palm trees. Sophie imagined herself lying on a lounge on the deck of that ship, sipping a cocktail, the breeze lightly blowing away any heat from the sun. She smiled. Next to it sat a diamond Audi key ring for the motoring enthusiast.

"Madam, would you like to place a bid?"

If only he knew. "No, thank you." Her purse was empty and her credit card maxed out.

A shove hit her back and Sophie reeled forward bumping into a beautifully dressed lady with diamonds suspended from each earlobe. One of Sophie's hands landed on her bust and the other expertly held the champagne flute aloft to avoid it dripping down the cleavage spilling from one of the latest Lilly Malone designer gowns. Sophie recognised the woman as a client. Weren't they all?

"I'm so sorry," she uttered, and removed her hand from the woman's breast and clasped her arm instead. A scowl erupted over the woman's face so Sophie quickly withdrew her hand and stood tall. "I do sincerely apologise. Are you all right?" she asked.

The woman ignored her but patted down her evening dress before returning to the group she was with. All held their noses in the air and spines stiff. One of the men was the CEO of a bank and notorious adulterer, if the rumours were correct. Sophie turned around to find out who'd so rudely pushed her. A joyous face greeted her, appearing not the slightest upset at the disturbance he'd caused.

The quick spin around caused Sophie to topple on her feet and feel unsteady. The room seemed to be spinning. No wonder after those three champagnes she'd downed in swift gulps. The gentleman held her firmly until she righted herself. Sophie squinted trying to get a better look at him and rubbed away the blur that had suddenly appeared in front of her eyes.

The man was all straight lines and sharp contours. If he'd been a painting he would be a modern piece, not an Impressionist artwork with its muted colours and smudging of contours. Or maybe a Picasso.

His dark hair was immaculately combed. His dark navy-blue pin-striped suit had crisp lines, and his face was smooth. Sophie longed to reach out and run her fingers across his cheek imagining it would feel like a baby's bottom. So different to Max's stubbly chin.

He looked amused as Sophie checked him out. "Would you like another drink?" he asked.

Sophie held up the glass in her hand. It still had a little sip left in it. "No. I'm good." The man smiled a broad, overly large grin encompassing his entire face. It irked he was laughing at her, but she didn't know what was so funny.

"I know you."

Sophie scrutinised him. He looked familiar but she could say that about most people present. "Yes. I'm sure we've met, Mr…?"

"You were ever so helpful to my fiancé, Miss Lovell."

"Oh, yes, I remember," Sophie's face brightened at the familiar name. "That was years ago. How is she? Is she here this evening?"

"No, I'm afraid she isn't. We parted ways. Since I'd paid for your services and don't any longer, she isn't lucky enough to continue to have a personal stylist."

Okay, that summed up the current situation in a nutshell.

She'd really liked Annabelle Lovell. Had briefly imagined they might be friends. Annabelle had always demonstrated fresh innocence and been such fun. Not at all like the other clients Sophie had at the time. She recalled Annabelle was creative with her clothing choices.

"I'm sorry to hear that," Sophie went to say his name but he hadn't provided it. "You're attending because….?"

"I'm on the board of the Museum. We've donated a piece tonight for the silent auction to support the charity."

It was a statement of fact and Sophie took a few beats to process it. He sat on the board of the museum? He'd been destined to marry Annabelle Lovell but now he wasn't. They had donated to the silent auction. The words swam around trying to gain traction and make sense. She sipped her drink and hiccupped from the fizz and that evoked further laughter from the man in front of her.

She found her tongue. "What item did you donate?"

With assured confidence, he placed his fingers at her left elbow and steered her toward the auction table. He pointed to a grotesque sculpture of something. She prayed it wasn't one of Max's. It didn't look like something he'd create, but what did she know about Max and his muse? She stared back at the fellow with her mouth slightly agape. He released a high-pitched laugh. Not enjoying being the amusement, she pulled herself together and considered the sculpture again.

God, it was ugly. Coloured a weird shade of pink, the shape was an odd sort of mouldy kidney with lumps and bumps, and a central opening. It reminded her of a woman's vagina especially with its folds and its beige tones.

"I take it you aren't a fan?" he enquired.

"It's different. I'm not sure what it's meant to be."

"I'm not sure you're meant to. It's designed to entice. To make you enquire and think laterally. To be different and evoke discussion."

"Okay," she said. "Well, I don't have a bid in the auction so it won't be coming home with me."

He whispered a number in her ear. Sophie leaned back, shocked and making no effort to close her open mouth. "It's worth that much?"

He nodded.

"That could feed a whole developing country, or build a new hospital here in Brisbane."

"That's why we're donating the proceeds to charity." Without her permission he pulled her across to a quiet corner of the room.

A waiter passed, and Sophie swiped another drink. A deep red Shiraz. She grimaced. Mixing drinks would not end well.

"I'm Fred." He kissed her, tongue and all, and held one of her hands. His palm was moist and clammy and hot to the touch. He had long, slender fingers and clean, square nails. Soft. Sophie couldn't help but picture Max's hands. They were workman hands that were rough and worn.

A waft of overpowering aftershave crept up her nose, and she sneezed. It was a bold smell and one meant to capture people's attention. Fred pulled away and the scent remained on her skin. He launched into a story about other notorious art pieces they'd had in the museum.

Sophie laughed and her insides buzzed with warmth from the wine, yet the walls around her closed in.

Chapter Fourteen

The crowd had thinned, and Max searched for Sophie's dark hair and red dress. A woman approached the bar and distracted him with a cocktail order. He ignored the flutter of eyelashes and the pout of her Botox-filled lips as he served the drink.

Max yawned and checked his watch. It was nearly midnight, and he hadn't seen Sophie for over an hour. With the mad rush of last drinks, he'd lost track of the time. Keeping an eye on the crowd he stacked dirty glasses and rubbed down the bench. It was time to call the evening quits. This bunch had had enough to drink.

A boisterous and high-pitched laugh travelled across the room.

Sophie? He stopped mid-wipe and held the cloth in his hand and stood on tiptoes to scan the heads of the crowd.

It was her. Her tall frame stood out at the edge of the dance floor. Sophie was doubled over with laughter before she rose up with her hands on her hips. Her voice drifted across the emptying space but he couldn't decipher the words. A dark-haired man laughed with her and held her arm in a way Max thought too intimate. The man leaned in close and whispered something in her ear. Sophie bent over again appearing to struggle to stay on her feet. Max's throat went dry.

"Mate, ready to start loading?" his offsider asked.

"Yep," he responded and stomped away, trying to keep Sophie in his sights. He didn't want to take his eyes off her, but he had to. For twenty minutes they packed the gear and cleaned the bar. Luke would be happy. They'd earned a killing watering this bunch. "Thanks for your help tonight," and he slapped the fellow on the back.

With his job done, he wanted to find Sophie. He rushed to the edge of the dance floor to find only a handful of men and women. None of them wore red. He waited outside the ladies loo but gave up after ten minutes. He shoved his way inside. "Sorry ladies. Sophie are you in here?" he yelled above the stalls. No response.

His heartrate accelerated and his chest tightened. There was no reason for him to be worried. What could possibly go wrong at a work event?

He rounded a corner fast and ran bang into Sophie engulfed in the man's arms. "What the hell?"

The guy had octopus arms. One was on her backside, the other caressing her back before they switched. She leaned into him and rested her head against his chest. Her eyes were shut.

What was going on?

Max gripped her forearm and tugged her away. Sophie's head sprang up and jerked while her body swayed. A strand of hair from her fancy French braid tousled about her face. He held tight.

"Ow," she said and yanked her arm out of his grip.

Max's fists balled. His feet were steady and apart and he was ready to punch this guy in the face.

Sophie slid to the ground and balanced on her knees with her back resting against the wall.

"Sophie?" his voice softened.

"He can look after me. Look after Gaby...lots of money...museum..." she mumbled incoherently.

"Who are you?" the guy in the suit poked Max in the chest.

"Who am I?" He controlled his roar. "Who are you?"

"I'm Fred and this is Sophie and we're getting to know each other." Fred looked Max up and down. "Hey, you're the barman. We'd like another drink. Sophie will have a champagne and I'll have a scotch on the rocks."

"The bar is closed. I think you need to leave."

"What? No. I'm leaving with her." He pointed to Sophie crumpled on the ground.

Anger swirled in Max's stomach and raged up through his chest. He shoved the man with a flat palm.

"Listen, it's been a long night. The event is over. Sophie isn't leaving with you. She needs to go home." Max worked hard to keep his voice even.

"Buddy, I don't know who the fuck you are, but be my guest. There's a roomful here tonight, if you don't get lucky with this one, try another, or better yet, steer her back in my direction. I wasn't finished yet."

Max relaxed his stance sensing Fred's defeat. "Get lost," he said.

Fred sauntered away and Max dropped to the floor beside Sophie.

"Soph?" he enquired.

"Go away," she whispered.

"What are you doing with that guy?"

"He said he'd look after me."

Tears rolled down her cheeks and Max wiped them away. "Why do you need him to look after you?"

"Because it's hard always being responsible. Being the only income earner. Being the adult." Her words gushed out. She sank her head in her hands and hid her face, and mumbled through her fingers. "He said I wouldn't have to work. Imagine that? Not having to ride the bus on a stinking hot day to get to the office, or sweating on payday and having most of it disappear on bills, and then watching my sister, sweet Gaby, struggle with being well and sometimes I can't make her better—" Sophie hiccupped and sobbed simultaneously.

Well, shit. "Let's get you home." Max lifted her under the armpits. A current jolted between them and Sophie's head shot up.

"Did you feel that?" she said with wide eyes.

"Yes." He wasn't going to deny it.

"When Fred," she flounced her fingers around, "touched me it didn't feel like that. Is it normal?"

"What?"

"That electricity every time we touch. That feeling, whatever it is?" Her eyes searched his.

"I don't know." He stared into her puffy eyes. The longing and burning desire he saw there scorched him and immediately all the blood in his body rushed south.

Sophie launched herself at him and latched her arms around his middle. Max lost his footing. Her bright red lips that matched her dress locked onto his. Those luscious lips tasted of sweet champagne.

Max's body quickly betrayed him and he kissed her back. Sophie kissed him deeply and pressed her mouth into his like she never wanted to let go. Her hands pushed into his back and forced their bodies together.

She pulled away to catch her breath but started to unbutton his collared shirt.

"Sophie, stop. What are you doing?"

"I want you'" she responded. Her pink tongue darted out to lick her lips.

Max pinned her arms to her side. Her eyes went so wide the whites were on display. She stared but didn't fight back. He held her in place and moved in to kiss her gently. This time with soft butterfly touches trailing down her neck and along her collarbone.

Sophie's body relaxed and she groaned, loudly. She wrestled her hands free and placed around his neck pulling his mouth back to hers. Their passion met. Sophie fumbled for his shirt again but Max stopped her.

"I want you," she repeated. She ran her hands over his chest and torso. She cupped his buttocks and pushed Max's groin to meet her pelvis. This was a Sophie he'd never witnessed before.

God help him, he could take advantage of her here, right now. He could do it, he wanted to do it. He pushed her back against the wall and held her in place with his hands and sucked in a lungful of air. He placed his hand on her thigh and caressed her leg until her skirt rode high and he reached her underwear. Lace. Argh.

Sophie's head leaned against his shoulder as he explored her bare skin. His other hand cupped her breast on the outside of her clothes but her chest fitted so tightly in the fabric he couldn't feel anything. He rubbed his fingers along the top rim and delved them deep inside her top until he discovered her nipple.

People walked past and watched them. Max came to his senses. What was he doing? This couldn't happen here. It was her work event. He was the barman. He grabbed her hand and her head rose from his shoulder. Without speaking he pulled her out the door.

Sophie stumbled on her high heels. She'd probably way too many drinks, and never ate as she'd promised.

"Are we going to your place?" she slurred.

"What about Gaby. Where is she tonight?"

Sophie grinned. "She's sleeping over at a friend's place, remember?" She traced a single finger along his arm and up his bicep. Goose bumps erupted over his skin.

"Okay," he agreed "To my place then."

When they reached the work van Sophie pushed him against the car and locked her lips on his again. Who was this woman?

She managed to open his shirt and swiped her hands over his chest and ran her fingers through his chest hair. He closed his eyes and savoured the sensation of her cool fingers over his hot skin. His body went rigid and his breath stuck in his throat.

He clutched one hand to each side of her face and drew her mouth to his again. He kissed her long, hard, and deep.

God, he wanted to taste every part of her. His hand slid up and into her panties. It pulsed with heat as he brushed over her curves. Passing headlights landed on them and placed them in a spotlight. The driver beeped the horn and hooted vulgarities out the window.

Max pulled away. What had gotten into him? He blamed hormones and a willing woman. But mauling her in the car park? His standards had slipped.

He placed his arm behind her back and helped her into the front seat. He tucked her in like a child, pushed the hem of her dress inside the door, and buckled her belt. Sophie didn't say a word. Her lids drooped.

He shut the door and paused briefly against it taking a few seconds to calm the blood in his veins.

As he drove off, Sophie leaned her head against the windowpane and fell asleep. Angelic, her face was peaceful in sleep. He recognised this Sophie. Max smiled and drove quietly and carefully so as not to wake her. He probably should take her home, but she'd be alone in her apartment.

His stomach churned at her comment. She'd said that creep could look after her. She meant money, of course. The guy was rich enough to provide for her needs. Perhaps she could live in a magazine home and have six children and be a member of the tennis club and assist the local charities if she married a man like that.

Such bullshit. Max knew a life like that didn't guarantee happiness. Often, it made you shallow and ungrateful. Life was too easy. He hated rich snobs who threw their money around and pretended to be someone important when they were actually insignificant.

He would be someone, but not because he had money or relied upon his parents. He would be a sculptor and recognised for his talent. His heart sank.

It was never enough, was it?

Girls like Sophie wanted security, comforts, and certainty.

He'd thought she might be different.

It sure made his raging emotions cool pretty fast. All along he'd known he couldn't measure up. Couldn't be what she wanted him to be. Max was too tired to think about it.

Tonight he'd look after her.

He could do that.

He'd take her home and let her sleep and offer her water and pain relief when she woke with a headache.

By then, he was confident he could look at her without wanting to rip her clothes off do all sorts of delicious things with her all day long.

Chapter Fifteen

Sophie rolled over and cracked open one eye.

Bright sunshine shot laser beams into her eye and she squeezed it shut. Her head throbbed, and her mouth was as dry as a cardboard cereal packet.

Where was she? Sophie sat up and groaned. She was in an unfamiliar bed in an unknown room. Her heart hammered. As hard as she tried to grasp memories of last night, none came, which exacerbated her nausea.

Noises floated in from outside the room. Crockery and cutlery clashing. A tap whooshing water, and the sound of music drifted in. It sounded like someone was moving around a kitchen. She prayed for signs of recognition as through squinted eyes her gaze wandered around the sparsely decorated bedroom.

Minimalist could be one word she'd use for the decor, lacking taste was more appropriate. Sure, the room had all the essentials. A futon bed, a wardrobe, and a corner timber desk was the sum total of the furniture. Surely, this was a single guy's bedroom. The wall colour was faded beige, and there were no personal touches. Books stacked high in narrow columns against the walls offered some insight into the room's owner. She leaned over to see if she recognized any of the titles. All of them were about art.

Max.

She flopped back on the bed, then shot up and searched for a mirror. Her image on the far wall reflected back at her. Oh God. Her hair was a tussled mess, and black mascara streaked across her cheeks. Before she could rub a finger across the bottom of her eyes, Max walked in.

He gave a weak smile and offered a glass of water and two Panadol. She refused to look at him, but took the pills and gulped them down with water. She handed him the glass and watched him from under her eyelashes.

He sat on the bed. "How are you feeling?"

Sophie felt like a caged animal while moisture pooled in her armpits. The room was suddenly too warm. She wanted to curl up and hide. "Not the best," she said, her voice rough and croaky.

"Is your head hurting?" he asked with a smile.

"Are you enjoying this?" she humphed.

He held up his hands palms out on either side of his head. "No. Why would you say that? I'm trying to take care of you. You had a few too many."

"Urgh." Sophie buried her head in her hands and held up the sheet to cover her chest. Panicked, she pulled the sheet an inch away from her body and looked down. Thank the Lord, she was still wearing the red dress. Which brought up another question: "How'd I get here?"

"With me, of course. You agreed to come home with me."

Sophie stared at him trying to read his expression. Max was a master at not giving anything away. He knew what she was thinking though because he smiled a wicked grin that reached his eyes and made them sparkle. Damn. He *was* enjoying this.

"Did we, you know, did we do anything?"

"What do you mean by anything?" he asked as if he couldn't guess what she meant.

Lifting the pillow that lay beside her, she whacked him in the face.

"Okay, okay. Not what you're thinking. We kissed a lot, and you did, um, try to seduce me, but being the gentleman I am, I resisted the temptation because *you were drunk off your ass.*"

Her hands flew up to her face and covered her eyes. "Oh, no. How embarrassing."

"Well, let's say I met a different Sophie last night." Max stood and picked up a shirt from a pile of clothes thrown haphazardly on the floor. "You ruined my work uniform trying to get it off me." He held up a white shirt with its buttons missing.

"I did that?" she squeaked and covered her head with the bedcovers.

Max laughed.

"It's not funny," she said remaining hidden. "I'm never coming out."

The bed depressed, and his voice was near her head. "Seriously, you have nothing to worry about. You drank too much, but hey, we've all done that. From your performance, I'm guessing you don't get pissed too often. Relax, its fine. You probably need some food though. I'm cooking a hangover breakfast. It'll be ready soon. Want to take a shower first?"

Sophie didn't remove her shield. She felt strangely protected from the outer world. "Okay," she croaked. The bed shifted as he left it.

"The bathroom is behind you. I'll leave out a fresh towel. Head to the kitchen when you're done."

***

Thank God for painkillers. As the water soaked away the rough layers of last night, the ache in her head eased and her body woke up. Dry and fresh, she couldn't bear to squeeze back into the red dress, so she searched for a large T-shirt. Sniffing the first she found, it passed the clean test.

The smell of bacon and eggs wafted into the room and her mouth watered.

"Did I eat anything last night?" she asked as she wandered into the kitchen from his bedroom as if it she'd done it a hundred times. She needed the situation to be less awkward, especially since she was wearing his shirt and nothing else.

Max tossed the eggs in a pan, collected toast and then said, "Early in the evening I reminded you to have something, but it was hectic at the bar, and to be honest, I don't know if you did." He turned the gas down before gazing at her.

Plonking herself down on a round timber stool at the kitchen counter, she covered her bottom half. He didn't say anything about her attire but his gaze roamed her body. Instead of focusing on him, she considered his home. "So, this is your place, hey?"

He nodded.

"Where are we?"

"West End."

They were in a small, timber cottage. The house was square with traditional VJ ply sheeting walls and pine floors. Unlike his bedroom, the kitchen exuded warmth and character, which was undeniably him. The sun's glow brightened the room with morning light. "Do you work and live here?"

Max served up their breakfast. "Yeah. The back room is officially my studio, but I drag my work into every available corner, as you can see."

An easel stood in one corner with a half-finished painting. Tubes of paint were tossed in the centre of the dining table, and scraps of paper lay on almost every surface in the space. She picked up the closest one, which depicted a partially-completed naked woman. Another appeared to be rolling hills in the countryside, and the last one she peeked at resembled an antique vase. The bins overflowed with other crumpled pieces "These are all yours?"

"Yep. They're muck around sketches. I play with ideas for either a sculpture or a painting, or maybe a drawing." He held up two plates. "There's not much of a deck but we can sit outside and eat." He didn't wait for her to agree, and moved toward a glass sliding door and a timber platform.

Following him, Sophie stepped onto a cleared space, no debris or other paraphernalia in sight. A simple wrought-iron table and chairs overlooked a ramshackle and overgrown yard. "Not big on gardening, then?" she teased with a smile.

He shrugged and shovelled food into his mouth.

Taking a bite, she savoured the salty bacon and softly scrambled egg. "This is so good. Thank you."

"I forgot the tea. No coffee I'm afraid."

Max returned with steaming mugs and Sophie said, "I appreciate you looking after me last night. You didn't have to. I'm not your responsibility."

Max's smile disappeared.

"What is it?"

"Well, I had to assist you last night. Otherwise you might have ended up with some guy named Fred. Do you remember him?"

Sophie gasped, and she dropped her fork onto her plate. "Oh my God. I do remember. Not all of it, but, did I... Did we... Were we kissing?"

"I'm not sure what happened. I found you with him. Fred," Max's lip sort of curled up in a snarl. "I think he had plans. All you kept saying was that he could look after you."

Sophie nodded. "I remember that. He offered me the world. Whatever that means. I'm guessing, in my drunken state it sounded perfect. The answer to all of my problems."

Max carefully put down his knife and fork so they sat parallel. He sat forward like he wanted to say something, his jaw twitching, but he didn't say a word.

"Show me your studio?" Certain she didn't want to hear what he might have to say.

They took their dishes into the kitchen already piled with dirty pots, pans, and glasses. "Want me to wash these up?"

"No."

He reached for her hand and led her toward the back veranda, which was an enclosed space that was obviously an addition to the old home. The floorboards were dark oak and the ceiling sloped at an odd angle. It was a long, narrow space with French casement windows lining one wall. A worktable sat aligned with the window, and blanks canvases were piled against the wall. All the surfaces were covered with paper, pens, paint tubes, and various cut up rags. The smell she'd detected on him all those days ago wafted around the room. The pungency tickled her nose and she sneezed.

She turned back toward the main part of the house. "Why don't you have any art hanging on your walls?"

"I can't bear to hang up work of other artists, and I don't want to look at my own."

"Weird," she said evoking one of Max's great smiles.

Clumps of dark orange clay sat on the far end of the worktable. An assortment of implements sat next to the clay: knives, blades, and dirty sponges. Mini-lumps were grouped around the edges of the table, but she couldn't discern what they were. Bright colours caught in her peripheral vision. In front of a chair—obviously the piece Max was currently working on—was an exquisite multi-coloured vase. She moved toward it.

"This is so beautiful and nothing like your piece in the gallery. Can I touch it?"

He nodded and she traced its smooth frame lightly with her fingertips. The blues and greens dazzled and reminded her of the ocean.

"I've been experimenting with glazed ceramics. I love working on sculptures, but they are more abstract and not to everyone's taste.

For some reason, critics don't always admire a headless woman or deformed physical state…but this," and he handled the vase as if it were a delicate child. "This is striking. Well, I think it is, and people love objects of beauty. What do you think?"

"I think it's divine. I'd love to own this. I'd run my fingers over it all the time." Their hands touched as they caressed the vase. His fingers were dry and calloused, a stark contrast to the smooth surface of the beautiful vase. She relished the diverse textures. He removed the vase and put it on the table. Their hands were still entwined and he grasped tighter as he closed the small gap between them by stepping forward. His light feathery breaths landed on her cheek and his hand tickled the seam of the shirt, nudging her naked thighs. A cavern of longing opened inside her; her groin pulsed until she couldn't bear it. Overwhelming need took over.

Do it, she willed Max. If he didn't, she'd jump him right here. Her breathing accelerated at the anticipation. She wanted him.

Max stared at her long and deep. Passion danced in his eyes as the evidence of his desire built. He turned and used her hand to direct her from the room, glancing back to maintain eye contact. She balled her other hand into a fist to prevent her from ruining another of his shirts with her over-zealous pawing. She intended to play it much cooler than she had last night.

As if there was a houseful of guests and they required privacy, Max slammed the bedroom door shut behind them.

Chapter Sixteen

"If your art doesn't pay, why don't you get a real job?"

They lay in his bed with the afternoon light streaming through the windows. Sated from amazing, energetic sex, Max circled Sophie's naked torso while she stroked her fingers across his bare thighs. The gentle, soft touch was almost more erotic than their lovemaking.

Being inside her was so much better than he'd imagined. At first, she'd been less wanton than last night, but after he'd pulled his t-shirt over her head—and damn if watching her walk into the kitchen in his shirt and nothing else didn't do a number on him—all her inhibitions went with the shirt, and she was insatiable.

Their first go was fast and wild. Both taking in as much as they could, as if there was a time clock they were trying to beat. Their second time was deliciously slow. He mapped her body with his tongue, tasting ever part of her until she was indelibly engraved in his senses. When he was working his way back to her breasts, she flipped him onto his back and proceeded to torture him with nips, nibbles, and a talented tongue. When she climbed on and rolled down the condom, he thought he'd explode, then he watched her lower herself onto him and he gritted his teeth to keep from letting go.

The promise of her was nowhere near as good as the reality, and he'd thought she held an infinite amount of promise.

Her question wasn't a jab. Her tone was light and playful. She wasn't judging or criticising him. He suppressed his sigh, tired of always explaining the same thing. Defending his choices. But this time Max refused to become defensive. He held her tighter and answered her with his lips a hairsbreadth away from hers.

"My work is art. I, along with every other artist, am subject to the whims of the market. It's difficult to manage, but I want to... No, need to, give myself wholly to it and that means sacrifice."

Sophie nodded her fathomless eyes wide. "But you work for Luke?"

"Yeah but only when he's short. I'm useful at late notice."

"You're helping as a friend, or do you need the money?"

"Both. The extra money is always handy, but there's never enough."

"Yep," she whispered, "ain't that true." Her hands moved up to his torso and she began stroking his sides. His body responded.

"If you won the lottery and had millions of dollars, what would you spend it on?" Sophie sounded miles away, dreamy and relaxed.

Before he could answer, her phone rang. She jumped up to retrieve it from her purse on the floor. Her butt cheeks danced and he got fully hard at the sight.

"I have to get this in case it's Gaby, even though she's not due home until about four."

"Oh, hello, Mrs Cartwright. How are you today?"

Max slid down into the bed and wanted to disappear. Talk about timing and making his guilt trip worse. He still hadn't confessed to being the son of Sophie's VIP client. He knew it was a lie of omission, but he'd wanted her to "be" with *him*. Not a Cartwright.

What a way to spoil a perfect moment.

Sophie sat at the end of the bed as she talked, wrapping the sheet around her as if his mother could see her. "Oh, that's wonderful. I'm so pleased you're happy with the collection I chose for you. You have some divine pieces. Yes, the shoes...." and then Sophie spent the rest of the conversation explaining reality. Trust his mother to put her through the wringer over footwear. He couldn't listen. He got out of bed, dressed and went out to make them tea. Sophie probably had enough alcohol for the weekend.

Their tea brewed before Sophie came out of his bedroom.

Her eyes were big and round. Max shoved the milk back in the fridge harder than necessary and the door swung back open. "Jeez, you've got nothing in your fridge." she exclaimed from behind him and the anger in him boiled over.

"Why do you answer a work call on a Saturday?" His words were sharp like steel.

She stared at him before answering. "Because they are important clients and if they wish to ring me on a Saturday I'm available for them. I can't afford it if they choose another stylist over me. The more I have on my books the better. You know what my responsibilities are. I don't have a choice." She sighed. "This one, thought is a real challenge."

Max pushed the mug of tea across the counter. He couldn't stop the question from tumbling out. "Why?"

"This client wants a pair of exclusive sneakers released a year or so ago. They released only one-hundred pairs, which sold-out in less than an hour. Lily Malone designed something similar since, but they're a slightly different style and shape and this client won't accept a pair of the new ones. I mean, how do I get hold of a pair of shoes that no longer exist?"

Max sipped his tea too fast and the liquid scorched his throat. "Tell her to go and get stuffed, and buy another pair of fancy shoes somewhere else."

"You know I can't do that." He ignored the entreatment in her eyes. "That would make her unhappy and my job is to do as she requests."

"But you said you can't do what she's asking." He held his hands as if to say, *and that's that.*

"That's correct," Sophie pronounced each syllable slowly and regarded him quizzically.

Max couldn't contain his derision. "How can you pander to these snobby, rich nobodies who are too lazy to source their own shoes? It's degrading."

Sophie stood up and the stool scraped. "It's my job. I'm paid well to keep these people happy."

"Is it worth selling your soul?"

Sophie's eyes narrowed and formed skinny slits.

Shit. He'd gone too far.

"That's a rotten thing to say, especially knowing what my life is like. Don't you think if I didn't have responsibilities I wouldn't want to be like you? Do whatever I like, earn money when I chose? But my life isn't that simple. I can't stay at home all day in this mess," she swept her arm wide to encapsulate the room, "and paint or draw or make objects for fun. I'm out in the real world working, doing the best I can." She placed her hands on her hips, and glared. "Fuck you if you find that distasteful." Turning, she left the kitchen.

Max heard Sophie moving around the bedroom. He knew he should go to her. Apologize. But he remained rooted to the spot clutching the hot tea.

He was well and truly a dick and he hated himself for it. Sophie had been thrust into a shit situation where her parents had died and she'd stepped up to care for her sister. Lesser people would have crumbled. Unlike him, she wasn't too proud to work a job she didn't love. He'd never do something he didn't love again. Sure, he might struggle financially and life was stressful at times, but that was part of an artist's life. No doubt, Sophie was a better person than he was.

An image of his parents popped into his mind. He did have a choice and despite his pigheadedness, he understood Sophie didn't. Regardless, he'd never ever give up his dream.

Sophie stormed out of his bedroom wearing her red dress and carrying her purse. He owed her an explanation, and he had to offer it now. She was already angry with him, it couldn't get worse, could it?

"Sophie, I'm sorry. I shouldn't have said those things. Please let me explain."

Instead of pausing as he expected her to, she continued on, flashed past him, opened the front door and slammed it on the way out.

***

Max holed up at home that afternoon. The phone rang, and he ignored it. His stomach grumbled, and he pretended he wasn't hungry. He worked, and didn't stop. As if his body was propelled by an external force, his hands didn't stop moving across the page. Pencils went blunt, and he'd grab another.

He finished a black and white pencil sketch of Sophie and then coloured her in another before painting a large over-the-top portrait in which she wore her red dress. Painting her luscious dark hair, he smelled its fresh and citrus scent and remembered the way it tickled his nose when they were tangled up in each other. Her porcelain skin dazzled, enchanting her dark, dancing eyes.

He worked on her painting until inch by inch the tension left his body. When he finished, she stared at him as he worked on more pieces. Ideas poured out of him and he created at least five unique vase designs he would produce later, and sketched more visuals in his notebook, trying them at different angles, shapes and designs.

He wasn't worthless. He worked hard. His parents' voices rang in his head. Max was determined his hard work would amount to something.

The business side of selling his art was not his forte, but somewhere, in the middle of his frenzy, he made a plan. His accountancy brain knew what to do, but he hadn't accessed those talents. He feared if he dipped one toe into those waters, he'd lose his balance and drown in the life he'd tried so hard to leave.

Exhausted, he fell asleep at his worktable.

Sophie's dark and stormy eyes bore into him as he drifted away.

Chapter Seventeen

Sophie's life had been a rollercoaster ride, but one she could usually manage. At times it was a train going too fast, and she needed to slow down. Sometimes she wasn't ready to embark and let it leave the station without her.

Frequently, there were too many unexpected dips, and she was desperate for the carriages to roll to a stop. But always, she managed to steer herself back on course. She did it alone. She prided herself on that. But now, her heart ached. She was off course, and she felt as if she'd lost sight of the destination.

She hadn't cried over a guy for a long time. Hadn't allowed herself to get close to anyone since her parents died. Sure, she'd had some disastrous dates, but she'd always been relieved when she found fault with them: they ate with their mouth open. They didn't like reading, or hated children. Some dates had been fine. Companionable. No fireworks, but no emotional tug of war.

Max, on the other hand, fucked with her.

Leaning against the window of the bus, tears trickled down her face. She'd let him in, believed they'd had common interests. She'd seen his caring, sensitive side, and they lit up like wildfire whenever they were near each other. She'd brought him to her home. He met Gaby, and had been kind.

That guy she liked. Really liked.

But that guy was only a side of Max,

The other Max. The asshole had said she was shallow and had sold out. He knew she did what she had to. She dealt with her responsibilities and got on with it. It wasn't an option for her to hide away and pretend she worked. Yeah, if she could, she'd have another job, but this one allowed her and Gaby to survive.

Sure, a lot of the time it bothered her. Then she'd research jobs she'd have loved and dreamt about, but they always required a drop in income. Anything art related, even the museum teashop or bookstore had meant a significant dip in earnings. Faced with ongoing education and health expenses for Gaby, she needed more, not less. It had been easy to wait for tomorrow, to put off her dreams and aspirations. There was always the future. But now the future loomed too close and nothing had changed. Time slipped by too quickly, and life made demands that required sacrifice.

Dreams did not pay the rent or buy medicine or put food in the fridge. She had to be the queen of reality, and because of it, they'd done more than okay so far.

She sat up taller and wiped the moisture from her cheeks. What a waste of energy wallowing was. Screw Max and his judgments.

On Monday she would speak to Inez about more clients for her books, and she'd solve that bloody sneaker problem. She slapped her thigh. She'd refocus. That's what she needed to do. Work and Gaby were the only things that mattered.

That didn't stop the itch in her fingers for dark and curly chest hair or recalling one sensual spot Max kissed on her neck that made her tingle all over. God, it'd felt good. Sophie crossed her legs for the rest of the bus ride home and tried to focus on what she'd make Gaby for dinner.

Chapter Eighteen

"Darling, why didn't you come to me earlier?"

Honestly, Sophie didn't know. Perhaps because it was her problem and she thought she needed to fix it on her own.

Sophie shrugged and sat in the comfy armchairs of Inez's office. "The requests are usually so easy. I understood straight away when Mrs Cartwright asked for those sneakers I was stuffed, and I wasn't honest with her."

"Of course, sweet pea. As if you would have been. The first consultation and she hits you with a whammy. We needed to lock in her collection, which you did, well done, and then sort this out." Inez put one finger to her chin in contemplation. "I know someone purchased a pair of those shoes at the time but who was it?" She stared out the window. "I chose the Mediterranean edition instead and love them, wear the pair all the time..." she mused. "Enrico," she screeched.

The door whooshed open against the plush carpet. "Darling, who purchased those Rubinesque sneakers almost two years ago? You know the ones with the diamonds along the sole edge and a variety of patterns and designs. They were one of our best designer runners. We need a size seven."

Enrico nodded. "Yep, I know the ones. I think it was Elise next door, or maybe Agatha from down the hall?"

"Go and find out. We need those shoes and now."

Inez's PA rushed out.

"Your book is pretty full, Sophie. I don't want to overload you, but we do have a new request we received today." Inez regarded her.

Bingo. Sophie clasped her hands together instead of power-fisting the air. "Oh, that would be great. I can attend to them today if that suits. I had a date to pull together a wardrobe for Mrs Ripoll. She's travelling to Paris at Christmas and needs a whole new winter ensemble. I can't wait to get started on that one."

"Okay, darling. Never forget you can say no."

Not on your life.

"This lady is the wife of a US politician and she's flown in without her luggage." Inez raised her eyebrow over the wacky red glasses she wore. Inez would never break a confidence or ask unnecessary questions. She'd never bitch about a client. Idle gossip was frowned upon and Sophie knew better than to enquire. She'd learned to accept situations: good, bad or simply weird. What did she care anyway? As long as they bought a wardrobe from Lilly Malone, that's all that mattered.

"Okay. She requires a new wardrobe of lovely Australian fashion. Hasn't she arrived at the opportune time with those latest summer dresses we have available?"

"She's going to love them."

Sophie gathered the necessary details for a visit with the American as Enrico blustered into the office without knocking. He held up a box and grinned liked he'd conjured gold.

"I found them," he yelled.

Sophie jumped up and rushed over to him. She grabbed that box and lifted the lid. Dare she hope? Inside sat a pristine pair of white diamond sneakers with pink trim and a garish and loud design Mrs Cartwright would love. Sophie lifted them out and held her breath as she checked the size. Seven. She dropped the box and hugged Enrico, and then Inez.

"Who had them?" Inez asked.

"Ruby. You should see the stash she has in her office," he exclaimed. "Next time I need anything," he exaggerated the word, "I'm going there first. She wasn't happy about parting with them. We owe her."

Lots of the personal stylists had their own amazing Lilly Malone collection, often snagging exclusive gear that didn't sell as well or had run its course and was heavily discounted. Sophie was one of the few members of staff who regularly rotated her clothes. The other stylists couldn't prize enough scarves, accessories, or special editions.

Inez nodded to Enrico. "I think one of the animal print leather handbags coming out soon might just do the trick." Inez's smile was wicked. "Thank you, wonderful job. Can you please confirm my lunch booking for four people at Marcos for one p.m.?" Enrico nodded and was dismissed. Sophie would thank him personally later.

She beamed at Inez.

"Problem solved, dear. Mrs Cartwright will love these and she will love you. Try to lock her in for a booking for the winter release."

Sophie floated out of the office clutching the box. She wouldn't let it out of her sight until safely delivered to her client this afternoon. But first, her mysterious new buyer waited for her at the Belvedere Hotel.

As usual, working for Lilly Malone was never dull. Working as an art curator couldn't possibly be so exciting.

Well, that's what she would tell herself anyway.

***

Silence stretched around the lavish dining room. Max hated lunching with his mother. Only she would deliver three courses on a Wednesday afternoon with fine china and sterling cutlery. As usual, she wore her resting bitch face.

"So, Mum. I've brought over a catalogue of new pieces I've been working on. These are different from my other sculptures." Max opened the portfolio and with one hand he pushed it closer to her. Azure blues and greens jumped off the page. It was hard to conceal his excitement.

He stole a glance at her. She continued to chew her prawn after delicately dipping it in the tartare sauce. Then she took a sip of wine.

"Mum?"

"Hmm?"

"I'm showing you my most recent collection. I've completed the first six pieces and I'm planning a series in this similar style. They are glazed ceramics. I think this range might sell well, and I'm proud of it."

She acted as if he hadn't spoken. She shuffled the linen serviette on her lap and dabbed at the corner of her mouth. Her lips curled as if she'd sampled something distasteful.

Fuck you.

"Diane might like these or the ladies at the tennis club? Or maybe for Dad's office?" His voice dropped.

"Let me understand this, Maximilian. You choose to abandon a lucrative accounting career at one of the top firms in the city where you were making a desirable income to *be creative*," she grimaced. "As I warned you, you would be unable to make a living out of such madness. Are you now confirming that I was right and you wish me to assist you by calling my contacts to garner some interest in your work?"

His fists balled in his lap. He sucked in deep breaths to prevent himself exploding.

"Would that be so terrible to help your son? Isn't that what family is for?"

"I paid for your exclusive private school education that allowed you to obtain a place at the most prestigious university in Brisbane. I paid for your degree, for the education you chose to throw away. I housed and fed you during your studies, and your father assisted you to obtain the professional position that hundreds of graduates applied for. It was because of us that you achieved so much. So forgive me if you wish to waste your life by pursuing a pipedream, and I'm disinclined to assist in that foolishness. I think we've helped you enough. You're adult enough to accept your responsibilities."

He'd heard them all this before, yet, for some ridiculous reason, he'd thought today might be different. That the unique vases he'd created in this collection might appeal to his snobby, cold mother.

If any other artist in Australia had created these pieces, she'd be ordering exclusives and recommending them to all of her friends. Her spite and bitterness ran too deep. In an attempt to keep his cool, and not fuel her fire, he flicked through the remaining pages, which was the only sound reverberating in the room. His mother placed her cutlery on her plate and it clinked against the china. He dared not look at her.

Max had a revelation. He was done with his parents. He'd tried to appease them for too long. He went out of his way to keep them happy to only be cut down. Wasn't a relationship a two-way street of give and take? They may not like his career choice, but couldn't they accept him because he was their child? Surely, they could handle the embarrassment at the country club on Sundays when mixing with their friends whose children were all living soulless and unfulfilling lives as bankers, lawyers, and real estate agents. He was sure she never mentioned him to her circle. She and his father were ashamed of him.

So be it.

He'd no longer excuse mother's prejudices because she'd grown up poor. She'd worked tirelessly to claw her way to the life she had, and if that worked for her, fine. But it was unforgiveable to shun him because he chose a life that didn't emulate her and his father's ambitions.

Loyalty had always kept him coming home, but he deserved better than what she dished up. As his mother advised, he'd made his choices, and he'd live by them.

Standing abruptly, his chair toppled. That caught his mother's attention. She'd expect an argument.

"Thank you for lunch, Mother. It was lovely."

Her eyes widened, and her mouth opened, and then the doorbell rang. She rose and left the table. Max took the opportunity to gather his belongings and look around, not sure when he next might return.

Echoes travelled down the hallway. Probably another of his mother's mindless friends.

He'd better make his exit, and fast.

Chapter Nineteen

Sophie never dropped in on clients unexpectedly. Today was an exception. Little bursts of fireworks pulsed through her body at the prospect of Mrs Cartwright's reaction to the shoes. She waited at her door and bounced nervously on her toes.

"Oh, hello, Sophie," Mrs Cartwright said, her smile tight.

Oh no. This was a mistake.

"I'm sorry, Mrs Cartwright if I'm interrupting. I have some exciting news." Sophie held her breath.

Mrs Cartwright glanced over her shoulder and then offered a curt nod.

Damn it. She should have telephoned ahead.

She followed Mrs Cartwright's stiff walk into the familiar living room. The air felt thick with tension. Sophie's dread built, and she swung the box in her arms.

"So sorry for bothering you, but I have a delivery I'm sure you'll be thrilled about..." Her words stopped short as she entered the room and there stood Max.

What the hell? Once might be a coincidence, but twice? Max gripped the high-backed chair so tightly his knuckles were white. Then, he reached for the full glass of wine on the table and gulped the remnants.

"What the fuck?" he asked.

Mrs Cartwright's glare was withering. Sophie stared at Max while his gaze raked over every inch of her. A red-hot blush crept up her neck and burned her cheeks. The shoes in her hands were forgotten.

"What are you doing here?" Sophie blurted.

"You two know each other?" Mrs Cartwright questioned.

All of the air was sucked from the room, and it became stifling and uncomfortable. Planting her feet to the spot, Sophie fought the urge to get the hell out of there.

"Maximilian, this is Sophie Williams, personal stylist for Lilly Malone…"

Max uttered the words in unison with Mrs Cartwright.

"And, Maximilian, who are you?" Sophie asked.

"What's going on here?" Mrs Cartwright enquired as Sophie and Max faced each other off. "He's my son."

Sophie's mouth dropped open and the box clattered to the floor. Max hung his head and had the decency to avoid eye contact. A cracking pain shot through her chest. She waited for his explanation. Surely, he'd have one. After a few drawn-out moments, he stood and a storm of defiance crossed his features.

Bugger him. She'd attack first. "Perhaps you'd like to explain, Maximilian?"

He took the bait. He gestured at the neglected parcel. "Don't you have a special delivery for Mother?" The words sounded wrong coming off his tongue.

"Um, yes. Here, Mrs Cartwright." Reaching down she scooped up the box. "I sourced those exclusive sneakers you wanted." Sophie plonked them into Mrs Cartwright's arms. After smiling at her client, Sophie turned to face Max and folded her arms over her chest and stood stock-still.

"Well done, Ms Williams." Sarcasm dripped off his words. "You've outdone yourself. Did you manufacture the shoes yourself? Pay someone a million dollars to hand over their pair? C'mon, tell us your secrets."

Max matched her stance. "Mother, you should be delighted with your personal shopper. This one goes above and beyond to deliver shoes."

"This isn't about shoes." Sophie said.

Mrs Cartwright removed the pair from their box and held them up, examining them in all their pink and diamond glory. "What are you two talking about? What about my shoes?"

"Forget the stupid shoes." Sophie flung her arms in the air.

"Oh, so now they're stupid shoes, are they?" Max jeered. "They weren't stupid when you were desperate to locate them to keep your VIP client happy. Ask her to do something else for you, Mother. Cook. Clean the house. These stylists will do anything to keep their customers happy. It's not only about fashion, handbags, and jewellery."

"That's not fair. You know I don't care about exclusive designer shoes or any of the other demands I get."

"Oh, but you do, Sophie. That's your job."

"At least I have one."

'Yeah, but I'm not selling my soul. I'm living the dream and being true to myself."

Sophie scoffed. She couldn't abide the diatribe coming out of his mouth. His words grated under her skin as a ball of fury formed in her chest. "But you aren't living the dream, are you? You scratch around for coins in your sofa to pay for your next takeaway meal. You have to work in a job you detest, helping out your mate to pay the bills your passion can't afford. Is that living? Always being tormented about where your next dollar is coming from?"

Mrs Cartwright turned to face Max. Sophie couldn't see her expression, but her hands were frozen holding the sneakers.

Max's nostrils flared, he breathed heavily, and his top lip curled. For the briefest flicker, Sophie felt rotten about the torrent of abuse spewing from her mouth.

He raised his hand and pointed at her, readying his vitriolic response, but Mrs Cartwright intervened.

"What are you two on about? This is a ridiculous display of behaviour." She turned to Sophie. "Max isn't starving. He can come here for meals any time, and we offer all the assistance he needs."

Simultaneously, they both turned on her.

"Please shut up." Sophie gasped and placed her hand over her open mouth. Oh no! The look on Mrs Cartwright's face caused another cracking pain to shoot across Sophie's chest.

Shit. She'd really fucked up now.

Max coughed. "Mother you don't have any idea what you're talking about. I don't have a spare buck to throw around, but that isn't your problem as you've made abundantly clear. I made choices and you don't agree with them. I can look after myself. This has nothing to do with you."

Mrs Cartwright dropped the shoes liked they scalded her.

"Mrs Cartwright, oh God, I'm so sorry. I'm angry with *your son* and I have no right to take it out on you. We're having a disagreement—"

Max sneered at her. "A disagreement. Is that what you call it?" He flung his arm at his mother. "Yep, fix the problem, Sophie.

You've upset your precious client. That's a dilemma, isn't it? Why don't you offer her an exclusive? Perhaps a special edition of, I don't know, a necklace or maybe designer swimwear? Yeah, that's it. A ridiculous and overpriced pair of bathers. They might have gold sewn into them so you can't actually get them wet but they'll look great at the beach and she'll be the envy of all her friends."

"You're pathetic."

"Get out," his mother screamed. "Both of you." Her body shook, and her face was mottled. She moved behind Max and pushed him in the back. Luckily, Sophie was spared the embarrassment of a hard shove. Instead, she received a malevolent glare, which got her feet moving fast.

Fuck.

Like recalcitrant schoolchildren, they were herded outside. The door slammed and they were alone.

A tsunami of rage swirled within in her body, and she clenched her fists to keep from punching him. She stomped her foot making her stiletto heel sink into the grass at the edge of the path. She couldn't walk away, not yet.

"How dare you? You have the audacity to accuse me of being shallow and fake, but you," she jabbed him in the chest, "you're a big fat liar. There is nothing worse. You can hurl all sorts of invectives at me, but at least I'm not dishonest. I'm sincere and genuine. I'm candid about why I do what I do. At least I have a reason, and a damn good one. I'm responsible for someone else. My sister. Who has no parents and a serious health condition. I'm her only relative, and the only one able to care for her." Sophie suppressed a sob, desperate to stay angry. "I'm not running away from a rich mommy and daddy choosing to *chase my dreams*. Everything I do is for Gaby. You can't say the same. And, *you* sure as hell aren't even be honest about it."

She watched his chest sink and his shoulders hunched. He peered off into the distance and let out a long sigh.

He's going to apologise and say he's sorry for being so goddamn disgraceful.

Sophie held her breath and waited for the words.

"Fuck you," he said, and walked away.

Chapter Twenty

Concentrating on the wet, sludgy clay didn't help Max turn off his brain. Feeling shit, though, was great motivation. His hands swept around clay, produced smooth lines creating ideas his mind hadn't caught up with yet. But it didn't silence the traffic in his head.

Was he selfish to choose his own path in life and not do what his parents wanted? He'd tried that, followed their advice, and had been the dutiful son. What kept gnawing at him though—was he happy? Had choosing the this path led him to the happiness he'd craved in a boring suit on his morning commute to work to sit in a square windowless box ten storeys off the ground? He wasn't sure how that felt, but it sure as hell wasn't happy.

Worst of all was the guilt about being dishonest. Sophie was right about that. He'd lied to her. Lied to himself. As he moulded the terracotta earth he justified his behaviour. He'd wanted to tell her. Tried to tell her. But didn't. She must hate him. Deservedly.

That night, he packed away his equipment and safely stored his new pieces to dry and made a decision. He'd brooded over it all day. If honest, he'd brooded a lot over the years. Perhaps mulling was his thing. But acting and not thinking was crucial.

Instead of waiting for the world to discover him as an artist, he would take his creativity to them. Max thumped his hand on the table. He needed to get serious. He revisited "the plan" he'd formulated the day before. As a qualified accountant, he was adept at business diagrams and budgets. Flowcharts had been his best friend. Why had he never applied his business sense to his own creativity?

He knocked his palm on his forehead.

Stupid. Stubborn. Thinking his amazing talent would speak for itself. Well, it had been astonishingly silent.

First though, he needed money. How did he think he could live without a regular income? An injection of funds was essential.

Pulling out his mobile phone that had been turned to silent all day, he rang Luke. "Hey mate, got any jobs going? Anything. Right now, this weekend or next week." He hung up and threw the phone across the room. When Luke had asked for help, Max had sucked in his pride and agreed. Now, when he reached out, Luke had a full schedule. Someone would fall sick Luke said and he'd let him know. More uncertainty.

He needed steady income if he was going to succeed.

Exhausted and momentarily defeated, he sank into the nearest chair. Enough life-changing decisions for one day. Tomorrow would be a fresh start.

***

When Sophie arrived home, she let the tears fall. Quietly, she dumped her bag on the nearest lounge chair and headed straight to the fridge for some wine. She'd bought this bottle hoping she and Max could enjoy it together. Bugger that. She'd drink it all by herself. She wouldn't think about him. She had more serious issues on her mind. Like her job.

Gaby came out of her bedroom into the kitchen.

"Hey," she said lazily, her eyes glassy.

Sophie sipped her wine and relished the warmth coursing through her veins.

Gaby tilted her head. "What is it? What's wrong?" Gaby asked.

Sophie had always held it together, and never cried around Gaby, regardless of how grim their life had been. Tonight, Sophie reached for Gaby and held her tight. Their roles were reversed. Sophie soaked up the delicious and familiar fresh apple shampoo her sister favoured.

And cried.

"Soph. Talk to me. What's happened?"

Sophie couldn't speak through her sobs. She gulped in deep breaths and tried, but only cried harder.

Gaby patted her back, and Sophie heard her sister mumbling reassuring platitudes. They sat like that until her mobile rang.

"I'm not answering it," Sophie hiccupped through tears. Gaby rose and Sophie heard her shuffling through her handbag until the ringing became louder.

"It's Inez."

Sophie bawled at the mention of her boss's name. She was so screwed. Inez would be furious. She must've found out about the scene at the Cartwrights.

Gaby swiped at the screen and answered the phone. Sophie jumped up and tried to steal it out of her sister's hands. Like a madwoman, her arms swatted and flailed but Gaby moved out of her reach. Too late, the call concluded and Sophie sank to her knees.

Gaby knelt down beside her. "Tell me what's happened?"

Sophie still didn't respond. She didn't know how she could put her afternoon into words. How to express that she'd made a terrible mistake, and their future was probably in jeopardy.

Gaby waited but Sophie didn't even want to look at her. She swept her palms across her cheeks to clear the tears and picked up the glass of wine and downed it in one gulp.

"It's okay. I had a bad day at the office."

Her sister looked at her like she'd gone nuts.

"I don't believe you. Inez was mad and she's coming right over."

"What? Inez is coming here?"

Gaby nodded.

"Fuck," Sophie uttered when the doorbell rang.

***

An hour later Sophie had stopped crying and felt more in control. She sat cross-legged on her lounge chair and across, facing her, were Inez and Gaby. Gaby had not left her side. She'd held her hand as Inez had stormed into their apartment and let loose her fury. That anger had lasted all of ten seconds when Sophie crumbled into tears. Inez's tone had softened immediately, and she'd embraced her like a daughter.

"You look wretched, child." Inez, childless in her late forties, could've been her mother.

What a waste. She'd have been a great mother.

Inez took in their humble surroundings in their under-decorated and sparsely furnish apartment. Then her eyes landed on Gaby. "Who is this?"

"This is my sister, Gaby." Inez's eyebrows shot up. She'd sat and instead of launching more apologies, Sophie had told her the *whole* story of her life, not the one Inez had been fed.

Inez hugged Sophie so hard the air had squeezed out of her lungs. Then Inez lunged for Gaby and did the same until the three of them were huddled in the middle of the tiny living area.

"Why didn't you tell me?"

Sophie shrugged. "I needed the job. I wanted to do well and didn't want you to think I had limitations. It was my problem, not yours, and not Lilly Malone's."

"You're fantastic at your job. Well, except today perhaps, but you're one of our most talented stylists, and you've kept this burden to yourself. We could have helped you, eased the load." Inez shrugged.

"Are you ashamed of me, Sophie? Is that why you didn't tell anyone?" Gaby asked.

Sophie gasped and turned to her sister. "No, absolutely not. My work had nothing to do with me being your carer." She addressed Inez and Gaby. "We know I wouldn't have been sent on any of those lucrative overseas jaunts, which helped grow my reputation if you'd known my personal circumstances. Those trips were hard on me, but they made me successful and in demand, and secured my job. All those evening events, and fashion shows, visits to clients after hours... If you'd known, I never would've gotten those opportunities." Sophie turned to Gaby and held her hands, "I've been eaten alive with guilt over the times I've neglected you, but I've done my best to care for you and work and hold everything together. We've done okay, haven't we?"

Gaby nodded. "I love you, Sophie. Mum's not here for either of us. You've been my mother and sister. I couldn't ask for anything more."

"I love you, too."

"Oh, Sophie, darling. I wish I'd known. Even if work was work, I could have helped in other ways. Cared for Gaby when you were away or cooked your dinners, or given you access to the hand-me-downs from the store. Anything."

"You've been an amazing boss and a great friend. I'm forever thankful for that day you walked into that crummy old bakery. I'll never forget my hair hanging around my face and the sweat dripping down my back and you saying that you needed an assistant and wanted me, right then. No one had ever wanted me before. I felt like Cinderella being whisked away to the ball that day. I can't ever repay you."

Inez laughed, the sound echoing around the small space. "Huh. I needed you all right. I was desperate that day, and you saved me. It was one of the best decisions I ever made. You've thanked me a million times over by working hard and making a fantastic addition to the Lilly Malone team. No more secrets."

Inez produced a bottle of deep red Shiraz from her oversized fashion bag and held it up. "Exactly what we need."

"You have a bottle of wine in your bag?" Sophie laughed.

"Darling, look at the size of this thing. I am ready for every occasion with this gorgeous Lilly Malone tote."

After Sophie opened the wine, Inez poured a beaker of the crimson liquid and handed it to Gaby. Sophie swatted her hand away. "Hey, you're a bad influence."

"I can be that naughty aunt who mothers groan about that take out their young charge clubbing and shopping for indecent clothing."

Inez handed the glass to Sophie instead. "Now, darling, what do we do about Mrs Cartwright? She *was* upset."

"Oh my God. I'm so sorry—"

Inez held up her hand. "No more apologies. How do we fix it?"

"I have another story about that. No more secrets, right?"

"Tell me. Sounds interesting." She winked at Gaby. "This is turning out to be most entertaining."

Inez sipped her wine and Sophie told her about Max. Inez's first words were, "He sounds dreamy. I must meet him."

"He is," Gaby said. "All dark and handsome. Moody too. Reminds me of a character out of one of my classic English texts." Gaby put her hand over her heart.

Inez lapped it up, but turned serious when she spoke of Mrs Cartwright. "It's my responsibility to fix this for Lilly Malone. She's a new and valued customer. I think it's best she's reassigned to a new stylist. You are too close, my dear, and we'll butter her up in creative and imaginative ways. She won't dream of leaving us for a competitor. You forget about her. Leave that messy business to me."

Sophie held back her tears. Someone stepping in to fix one of her problems felt like a dream come true.

Today's lesson: she didn't have to manage on her own.

A sudden weight shifted off her shoulders, and she sat back as Inez told Gaby funny stories about the fashion industry. Her boss loved a captive audience, and seeing Gaby's cheeks flush red a number of times she amped it up even more.

"You, young lady, are on a forced sabbatical. Three days at least."

Sophie protested. "Relax, it'll be paid leave. I think you've accrued enough, what do they call them? Flexi-hours? To warrant a couple of days of R and R."

"What will I do with myself," Sophie moaned.

"Go to the museum, of course," her sister piped up. For Inez's benefit, she added, "That's her favourite place in the world."

Sophie rarely revealed her inner most desires to anyone, but with a tongue made loose from a few glasses of wine, and Inez's unfathomable support, Sophie said, "Yeah. If life had been a little different, I might have pursued a job in the arts. Maybe a curator, or historian, or something similar. Whenever I can I love to wander about the museum."

"Hmm," was Inez's response. "My girlfriend is a curator. I'll have to arrange a coffee."

"Did you say curator?"

Inez nodded as if Sophie's whole world didn't hang on that word. "She's well-known in the industry."

Dumbstruck, Sophie sat mute but Gaby squealed before jumping up and saying all the things Sophie wanted to.

"Can Sophie meet your girlfriend? She's desperate to work in that area."

"Of course, darling. I'll get straight onto it."

Chapter Twenty-One

"Hello, young man. Did you make these?"

Max nodded. "They're all my creations."

"They're beautiful. How much is this one?" the lady asked. She was wearing a floral print dress and used a walking cane. She pointed to one of the tall glazed vases. Max stood behind his stall at the local weekend market.

Max advised her of the price and her hand crept to her mouth and she actually snorted. "Too expensive for me, love. I'm a pensioner," and with a friendly wave she wandered off.

Maybe he pitched to the wrong demographic. The local markets filled with handicrafts and trinkets—most of which were for a few bucks—was probably not the most lucrative place to sell his stuff.

He fiddled with positioning the five pieces still on display. He moved one to the front only to move it back again moments later. Maybe he'd gotten lucky this morning with his early sale. A woman in activewear trolled the booths and forked over the money for the classic cut ceramic bowl in what he hoped would become his signature colours. One of his favourites. He hoped the sale hadn't been a fluke. Max wished she'd bought two.

He shaded his eyes. A blazing sun sat high in the sky and tinged his skin where the sunshade didn't protect him. Only a few more hours and he'd declare this experience a disaster and remodel his business plan yet again. It would appear these local markets didn't work for high end products.

Opening his sketch pad with his pencil poised, he waited for inspiration to strike. His hand remained still.

"Max," a voice yelled and two arms encircled him from behind. "It's so great to see you."

He turned and was shocked to see Sophie's sister. "Hey, Gaby. How are you?"

"I'm good. Sophie's in the toilet. The queue was huge and I spotted you." She placed a flat palm to his chest. "I'm not sure Sophie will be pleased. She's livid with you. Been moping for days, plus she's in trouble at work, but that has been sorted. Her boss, Inez, is pretty cool..." Gaby rambled on and Max had trouble keeping up.

"Gaby. There you are. I couldn't find you..." Sophie's words trailed off as stood in front of him. "Oh. Max. Hi." Her polite civility sliced through him. Of course, it'd be like that. After tearing into each other in from of his mother, of all people, he couldn't expect a warm welcome. Sophie avoided looking at him and turned to his table. "Wow. You're selling your ceramics here at the markets."

"You made these?" Gaby asked. "They're gorgeous. Our mother loved vases. She'd have bought all of these and placed them around our home.' Gaby looked wistful.

Sophie trailed a finger down the smooth surface on the tallest vase and agreed. "Yeah, she would have loved the dazzling colours, the shape, their uniqueness… They are truly amazing."

Max stared at her as she spoke but didn't respond. To be honest, he was dumbstruck. He hadn't seen Sophie since their blazing row over a week ago. Now she appeared like an apparition before him with the sun surrounding her like a halo around her dark locks. Those black eyes peered at him with intensity and he shifted in his seat. She took his breath away.

"Sophie's had this week off work," Gaby said, filling in the silence and interrupting his reverie, "and she's so relaxed."

She wore denim shorts and a white tee, and she didn't look like a rod had been shoved up her back.

It wasn't the clothes he focused on though. Those legs. He remembered what they felt like wrapped around his hips as he moved inside her. He closed his gaping mouth.

He'd never seen her so relaxed, except for maybe that one time she lay under him and her face shone with a light sheen of perspiration and her eyes had been dreamy and filled with lust.

Max's mouth went dry. He reached for his water bottle and as he drank, he knew he needed to apologise, and began to form the words when a man approached and Max became distracted in sales talk. Sophie and Gaby stayed near the stall while he did his best to encourage the man to part with his hard-earned money. No sale.

"Sophie, I love this one. Can we buy it?" Gaby exclaimed

Sophie paused.

An opportunity. Jump in and say sorry. Instead, the silence drew out and he wondered if she expected the vase for free. Or worse, she didn't want it and was reluctant to say so in front of him.

"That's a great idea. Mum would have adored this one." Sophie touched the patch of bright pink at its base.

His lust going wild only moments before cooled immediately and Max's stomach became a fortress of tightly strung knots. Handouts? Pity? That's all he thought of. "I don't need your charity," he muttered gruffly.

"What?" Sophie stared, her forehead creasing. "It's not charity. We want to purchase this one. Is it for sale?"

His features turned stone hard and his heart went cold. "Yes, to genuine buyers only not people feeling sorry for me."

Sophie jutted out her chin. "Maximilian Cartwright, you're as stubborn as a mule and that's the most polite way I can say it. Will you sell us this vase?" Her voice was clipped.

"No."

"What's wrong with you?" Gaby asked. She stared up at him with her puppy dog eyes. Max held strong, excepting his damned left eyelid kept twitching. Let them think I'm cruel and then maybe they'll stay away from me and feel sorry for someone else. His stomach cramped and a frisson of unease coursed through him.

"C'mon, Gaby, let's go." Sophie turned away and tugged on Gaby's arm as she continued to stare at him. Shame washed over him. Gaby's cheeks flushed before she gazed down. Max looked away and couldn't watch them leave.

He was a verified ass.

Despite his appalling behaviour, fate was on his side after lunch, and he sold two more pieces. The sales lifted his mood. Since the exchange with Sophie a lump had formed in his chest and he hadn't been able to dislodge it. As the day drew to a close, he was becoming desperate. With confidence he hadn't displayed in the morning, he eye-balled every customer. If they so much as smiled at him, he offered his most impressive sales pitch to no avail.

Dusk approached and most stallholders had packed up and gone home. The few owners that remained wiped down tables, dismantled marquees or sat with their neighbours downing a cold beer.

Max didn't move. His three remaining pieces remained in prominent position. A man approached and their eyes connected. Max's heart thudded. This was it, his last sale. Instead, the man dumped his old newspaper on the trestle table and kept moving. Max picked it up and decided to read it. After he turned the last page he'd pack up too.

The pages flicked over to the classifieds, and he spotted an ad.

Bookkeeper required. Work from our offices one day per week. Medium-sized family company.

Excitement pulsed in his belly and Max rushed to pack up.

Chapter Twenty-Two

Sophie paused as she stood on the top step outside of Inez's home. She could hear Gaby breathing behind her.

This was their third dinner together this week.

She'd always trusted and liked her boss, but since she'd told Inez the truth, she'd proved to be an amazing friend.

Overnight Inez became a surrogate mother. Not only to her, but to Gaby as well.

Their house was the best on an otherwise ordinary street filled with family homes. Bikes were scattered in driveways along with other toys and the trees had swings hanging loose and blowing gently in the breeze.

If Sophie had to guess where Inez and Evelyn lived, top of the list would have been a fancy, modern apartment with stunning views overlooking the Brisbane River. The floor would be covered with shiny white tiles she'd seen in every client's mansion.

Sophie was getting used to being wrong. The home was impressive and yet understated. It might have been grand, but it wasn't a house, it was a home. Like the two women who lived there, it was warm, welcoming and not in any way ostentatious. While the walls were muted the trimmings were bright. Photographs were hung with care with not a gold-rimmed frame in sight. Everything was soft, inviting, and elegant. Decorating done well with family and friends in mind. Sophie had loved it from the first moment she'd walked in the front door.

"What are you doing standing there? Darlings, do come in." Inez kissed her on both cheeks and ushered them inside. The woman had a sixth sense and somehow knew Sophie was on the doorstep ruminating.

For so long, Sophie had fended for herself. Made the hard decisions, and tried to act like a grown up when she hadn't felt like one. Like a burst of fresh air, Inez and Evelyn had entered their lives.

The pair of them were intractable and relentless, but genuine and sincere. Sophie had never felt more loved.

In addition to the meals, there had been phone calls and drop ins and deliveries of treats that Sophie could never afford. The local French patisserie had delectable delicacies Sophie only ever gazed at as she ordered her croissant. Some mornings, she'd open the front door of the apartment after receiving a text message, and there would be a picnic basket of coffee and the most expensive of French tarts. Never one or two, but a box, including the special low sugar variety for Gaby.

This dinner was different, though. No doubt it would be fun and the company wonderful. But Sophie had had conversations with Evelyn about her work as a curator. Some of them lasting hours and Inez had had to push her out the door to take Gaby home to bed. The fire that used to burn in Sophie's belly had been reignited. Those conversations had got every nerve end tingling, and made Sophie believe her dreams could come true.

Usually she'd throw on something comfortable and not designer Lilly Malone to wear to a dinner with friends. But tonight, well, this was important.

Sophie looked down at her outfit. After an agonising few days and numerous telephone calls to Inez for advice, Inez had visited yesterday and rescued her, once again.

"Goodness gracious, Sophie, you'd think you were meeting the Queen," Inez had exclaimed. "I appreciate someone making the effort to look good, but you must feel good too, darling, don't forget. Let's try these on."

Like a scene in a movie, Inez plucked an ensemble of clothes out of her bags. There were dresses and jumpsuits Sophie could personalise with her own accessories.

She'd paraded them like one of the fashion models for Gaby and Inez who had oohed and aahed at all the right moments. Sophie settled on a pale pink vintage jumpsuit. The colour reminded her of her mother's roses. It was not overdone or flashy, but could be suitably dressed up with pumps and gold bangles that would match the gold buttons featured down the centre of the dress.

"Perfect," Inez had commented. "Now you'll have to find somewhere to hang all these others. They are yours to keep."

Gaby squealed and immediately leapt up to hold them against her frame to see if they'd fit.

Sophie stood gaping. There were at least thirty items of clothing. Sophie opened and closed her mouth but no words came out.

"Now before you go saying you can't accept or you feel bad or some other thing, let me tell you that if you don't take these clothes they are going to be placed into the charity bin at the end of the street and some other quite deserving person will collect them and enjoy wearing such beautiful pieces. That worthy person should be you."

Inez didn't wait for a response. She rose from the lounge and headed to their small kitchen.

Sophie hadn't noticed Inez had any other bags, but from somewhere she produced another three or four that she proceeded to unpack. They were filled with groceries of tinned food, boxes of cereal and cake mixes, and fruit and vegetables.

Gaby went to Inez and pulled her into an embrace. Tall Inez engulfed the tiny Gaby and they stood like that for a heartbeat. With her thumb, Sophie wiped away the solitary tear that rolled down her cheek.

Her chest constricted but not in its usual way. Normally, a shooting pain would trek its way across her chest when she realised they were down to the last dollar in their bank account, or especially when Gaby was unwell and Sophie was the only person to make her sister feel better. No. This wasn't one of those pains. This was a warmth that started deep within and spread throughout her body.

Sophie didn't make any comment to Inez about the bags of food. Some things were better left unsaid.

Of all Inez and Evelyn's gifts, tonight's was one of the grandest. Sophie was about to meet Mr Simmonds, director of the museum, along with a number of other members of the team. Sophie was unsure if she was about to meet two people, or twenty. Expect the unexpected, she mumbled under her breath.

Tonight was the night.

Gaby squeezed her hand as they entered Inez's home.

***

"Oh my God, darling, you were amazing," Evelyn gushed.

The last remaining guest had left and they were alone. They were seated at the grand oak dining table and picked at the leftover food.

"You truly were, Sophie. Well done, pet." Inez smiled as she stabbed at a ginger and honey prawn with a fork. "They were suitably stunned by your knowledge of the arts. You've done your homework, girl."

"It's hardly homework when it's something you love. I've read everything I could get my hands on for years now. Borrowed art magazines and books from the library, visited every exhibit at every private gallery, read the papers and blogs, and social pages."

"I underestimated you," Inez remarked.

Sophie beamed, but her stomach rumbled. She reached for a dumpling and devoured it quickly. "I'm starving. I was too nervous to eat before and then too busy talking. They're such nice people and so passionate about what they do. Imagine working with such objects of beauty and creation all day." She chomped on some spicy seafood noodles.

"Can you imagine it, Sophie? Because you'll be working at the museum. It's only a matter of time. As I've mentioned, John has a retirement plan. He's already wound down his days, and I think he's enjoying his leisure time. He spoke to me about putting you on immediately, probably being the general helper in the start, doing anything and everything but that gives you time to learn the ropes. Like an apprenticeship, I'm guessing. Then, eventually, he can retire happily knowing the museum is being well looked after. By me, that is." Evelyn chuckled at her own joke.

Sophie rested her fork gently on the table.

"Well, that's not a happy face," Inez said.

"Of course I want the job, but I know how much the lower positions pay, and we can't live on that." Her appetite had vanished.

"Oh, I know sweet girl. We've thought of that. We understand." Evelyn reached across and held her hand.

For a brief moment, the thought of being adopted flashed into Sophie's mind. How ridiculous. A person was not adopted at the age of twenty-five. Her brain was turning to mush.

"Inez and I have talked about it. The hours at the museum are demanding but not intolerable, but definitely a sizeable pay cut. Therefore, Inez will keep you on as a stylist on a part-time basis to make up the difference. Of course, she'll assist managing your diary so you can fit in both schedules."

Evelyn sighed and sat back in the dining chair. "It's not perfect, but like most jobs, you have to work your way up and in. The museum isn't any different. It needs to become a home to you. A place you know intimately. You need to know its operations, it's heart, its purpose. You will, but that takes time. Of course, when I started money was of little consequence. I was living at home and didn't have many expenses. But it does pay as you progress, and you will."

Silence filled the room as Sophie's mind ticked over. She looked up at the expectant faces all peering at her.

"It's perfect. I'm so used to working hard. It's a perfect solution." She jumped up out of her chair and raced around the table to embrace both women. As she hugged them she felt their bodies sag with relief.

"Unlike before, you'll have support. No more being stubborn and going it alone. We want to help you. Want to see you succeed. You deserve it. If our delightful Gaby is going to go to university and study those ghastly bugs and diseases or whatever she chooses, you'll continue to need help," Inez said.

"I've been thinking about that too," Gaby said. "It's time I got a job."

Sophie leaned forward to speak. Gaby held up her palm. Sophie shut her mouth. Her sister was getting older and she needed to remember to treat her like an adult.

"I'm old enough. Most of my friends have jobs and it's even more important I help share the load. I've been looking around and I'll start applying, and hopefully the load will lift a little off you, Sophie."

Sophie's throat tightened and she choked up, but managed to say, "Aren't you the best?"

"How fabulous, darling. Your dear parents have instilled the most wonderful work ethic in both of you." Inez turned to Evelyn and her voice rose, "Roberto, who owns that dear little café on the corner of our street and serves the most delicious blueberry bagels by the way, I think I heard him say the other day he is looking to hire someone. Tomorrow we'll introduce you."

"Is there anything you two can't do?" Sophie asked.

Both women went quiet. Then so in tune with each other, they simultaneously broke into laughter. "Probably not." Inez said. "Eat these leftovers please. This Asian banquet cost a fortune and I don't want to be eating fried rice for a week." They all laughed. "Let's toast to the two wonderful young women who have entered our lives, and to the future. It is bright."

Chapter Twenty-Three

Max was pleased with himself. Who'd have thought he could fix his own problem? Not his mother, that's for sure. But, he'd done it.

Well maybe some tall and lanky woman with dark hair and porcelain skin had given him a well-deserved push. But nonetheless.

Like a child, he wanted to skip down the street with joy, but decided to take in the world around him.

For once, instead of moping about his situation, he'd taken action. Things were looking up. If he wanted life to be better, he had to create it. Sophie had been right. He wasn't selfish though, that was harsh. Perhaps unmotivated and stubborn was accurate.

Someone had been looking out for him last week when that man dumped his paper on his stall table.

At a little after five pm, the sun was shining and the streets were starting to fill with workers finishing for the day. The sun had lost its heat and now radiated a yellow glow over the city. Max walked along the river bank heading towards home.

The water in the Brisbane River rippled in the light breeze and City Cats sailed past. It was idyllic: boats chugging on the river, the steel bridge spanning its width up ahead, birds flying overhead and the sounds of a city coming alive at dusk. The lights came on illuminating the streets, and the stars began to sprinkle the sky.

It'd been a long time since he'd felt a sense of achievement after a hard day's work. And that was exactly what he'd done today.

Day one at the small family owned party supply business was done and dusted. They'd been managing their own accounts for years, but with a recent expansion and an increase in staff, they needed expert assistance. Him.

Funny. He'd dreaded a return to the MYOB accounting software and balance sheets, but in between paying the wages, the whole team had shared a cake for morning tea to celebrate someone's birthday, and he'd had brief chats with staff over the coffee machine. He hadn't realised how much he missed company, and meeting new people. Sure, the business wasn't really his thing—they supplied the residents of Brisbane with helium balloons in all colours and designs, along with poppers, streamers and every conceivable item a person would want to have a party. As a family business they were passionate about their company. They didn't subscribe to a corporate mentality. Their enthusiasm was contagious, and it'd been fun. Plus, he'd been paid.

Max ran his fingers along the edges of the notes folded in his pocket. He would receive the same next week.

As an added bonus, the family had introduced him to a friend who runs a photographic studio, *Francis Creations*. Their friend was too busy running shoots, and the schedule of his team of photographers to manage the books. He'd hired Max immediately for one day per week.

In less than seven days, he'd gone from no regular income, to two permanent days per week.

Max walked lighter. But he was under no illusions, and wouldn't get ahead of himself. A million dollars was not about to drop into his bank account. But he had money to cover his basic bills, his living expenses, and his bread and butter: paint, clay, brushes, sketch pads, kiln fees.

Max quickened his step. He was busting to get home and write down a new sculpture idea he had before it disappeared.

But first, he spied a green grocer. Another different idea sprouted.

Outside were large bunches of vibrant flowers in all varieties. Fresh flowers made him think of his mother. She loved flowers. It was a secret indulgence of hers that she engaged in frequently.

Despite what he'd said the other day, he hated that he'd closed the door on his family. It had bothered him ever since. Today he'd been surrounded by a family that supported and loved each other. Of course, no family was perfect. But observing them had caused an ache in his chest. A realisation that his relationship with his parents could be different. He knew they weren't going to change, but his dad was all right. He was more approachable than his mother and easier to talk to.

If he wanted the relationship with his parents to be different, he had to be the better person.

A bunch of bright yellow daffodils stood out. They sat in a bucket crowded on all sides by carnations and roses and lilies. He lifted up one bunch of the long green stems. Everything seemed clear to him. He'd make amends and buy these for his mother and grab a bottle of wine for his dad and go and see them later tonight. He would have to learn to accept that the flowers might be too wilted and the wine not quite expensive enough, but the effort would count.

Max inhaled the scent of the flowers and out of the corner of his eye he saw a pink gerbera. He touched its petals and they were fragile in his thick fingers. Should he buy a second bunch and visit someone else?

He imagined Sophie wasn't given flowers often. He deliberated but pulled his hand away and went inside to buy the wine.

His legs felt heavier as he walked now. The dusk sky less vibrantly pink.

Sophie. What was she doing now? Overseas fawning at another special client? Or dropping off an entire collection of cocktail wear to an exclusive mansion in the suburbs, or maybe she was getting spruced up for another fashion event.

The sun sank behind the clouds and the world turned grey. All of a sudden the flowers were cheesy and a pathetic attempt at apology and he no longer felt inclined to forgive his parents. Not today. They hadn't called him to make amends.

Max dumped the daffodils into the nearest garbage bin.

Now he only wanted to sit on his couch and drink a cold beer.

He pulled out his phone and called Luke. Catching up with his best mate sounded like a much better idea.

Chapter Twenty-Four

One month later

Sophie lifted her head at the squeal of tyres. A car screeched to a halt dangerously close to her and she yanked her legs back inside her vehicle to avoid being run over. "Idiot," she said as she collected her purse from the passenger seat.

The shiny, blue Audi had squeezed into the adjoining spot leaving her hardly any room to get out of her car. She grumbled profanities under her breath and she sucked in her tummy before sliding out.

"Max?"

He stood next to the fancy European car holding a bulky object. He glanced up at his name and pushed the button to close the boot while his knee held the package in place. With wide eyes he moved around to the front of the car and placed the item on the bonnet.

Sophie's heart hammered against her ribcage. A blue suit hugged his body and stretched across his broad shoulders. His dark locks were slicked back, and his beard was neatly trimmed. And, oh God, the smell of him: methylated spirits and glue mixed in with vanilla scrub and eau de toilette. The heady combination had her head spinning. Sophie looked between him and the car. Max in designer clothes and driving an Audi.

"Is…is this yours?" she pointed at the car. Sophie hadn't seen or spoken to Max in over a month and her first question was about a car. Stupid.

Predictably, he answered with his usual cut-throat derision. "Does it matter?"

"No," she answered.

"Is that yours?" he nodded towards her car. She swore she saw his eyes twinkle.

"Yep. She's a beauty isn't she? I finally have my own car. It isn't much but it's reliable and Gaby is learning to drive, so I needed one." Sophie heard the pride in her voice despite the car appearing even more aged and the paint even duller sitting next to the meticulous new Audi.

Comparisons didn't matter. Sophie loved her car.

Inez had helped her. Ironically at the time Sophie was looking to purchase a car, Inez had a friend who was upgrading to a newer model and wanted to offload the old version. The metallic grey Saab had been well cared for and wasn't old in her books. Sitting in the driver's seat—if she closed her eyes and inhaled deeply—she could still smell the new leather scent. She'd never thought she'd own a car like this. It had built-in GPS and cruise control. With Inez acting as negotiator, she'd scored a great price.

"Congratulations," Max said and nodded.

"What are you doing here?" Sophie cut to the chase. "You don't look like you're dressed to work the bar tonight."

Lilly Malone was releasing an exclusive handbag collection this evening. Their first in a number of seasons.

He shook his head. "Not tonight. I'm a guest." The words hung in the air.

"Hey, my man." Luke came up behind them and slapped Max on the back. "You're here. If I can't keep up with the demand for drinks tonight, you're my backup. I'll come and find you even though you're all trussed up for a party." The two men laughed ignoring her.

Sharp prickles of heat crept up her spine. A guest? She was desperate to know more but also wanted to run into the safe confines of the function room of the Treasury Casino. Shuffling the designer clutch—one of tonight's new products—into her other hand, she waved farewell and moved away. "See you inside," she called behind her.

Sophie headed straight for the bar to take the edge off. All of a sudden, her throat was parched. An unfamiliar barman served her an elegant flute of French champagne. She really was getting a taste for this expensive alcohol. Inez and Evelyn drank it like soft drink.

The bubbles tickled her nose and the cold liquid slopped down her throat loosening her tight shoulders.

She stayed where she was and leaned against the bar. It was prime spot to observe Max as he walked across the cavernous room toward the auction table. His knees buckled under the weight of the object he carried.

Lucy, another stylist, approached Sophie and interrupted her fantasising. Sophie had been undressing Max in her mind. She could remember every detail of his broad chest...

Lucy pulled her back into reality and they chatted and admired each other's bags. For once, Sophie adored the range. The colours and patterns were less outrageous than usual and more suited to the ordinary woman. A range for all tastes. Perhaps Inez was softening in her old age. More likely she'd identified a gap in the market and gone for it with her usual gusto.

Lucy wandered away to mingle and Sophie watched Max. She couldn't tear her eyes away from him.

The package he'd carried now sat centre stage on the table designated for the night's charity auction. He bent at the waist and carefully unwrapped one corner and then the next. The outer wrapping was peeled away with such care it caused shivers to race up her spine. She remembered those fingers and their magic. She could feel them on her bare and moist skin.

He unwrapped a glazed ceramic piece. One she hadn't seen before, but was unmistakably his creation. Sophie's breath hitched. This one was tall and grand. Along with the expected azure blue and green intermingling together throughout, a tinge of the bright pink she'd admired in the piece she'd wanted to buy, but the jerk had messed that up too.

One slash of the distinctive colour ran up the length of the vase and moulded with its curves. Max stood back to admire it like he'd not seen it before either. People drifted over to the table.

The piece was one of his finest.

A Lilly Malone model sidled up next to him and clutched tight to his elbow and leaned so close her breath must have brushed his cheek. Her other hand held one of the petite camel-coloured leather bags available for order tonight. The colour ensemble was striking with her vanilla-blonde hair and vintage red lipstick. Beauty personified. But all Lilly Malone models were stunning. Sophie'd never cared about the catwalk gorgeousness before, but that was before one of the most attractive chose to drape herself all over Max.

Sophie was quietly seething. The floor-length deep burgundy dress with full skirt and low V cut the model wore revealed her voluptuous, surely paid-for, breasts. The high split showed off a slim tanned leg. Nothing left to the imagination there. She could have sworn Max dipped his head to get a better look.

She gulped the remainder of her drink and ordered another. Don't kid yourself, Sophie. All of the beautiful women in the room would be attracted to Max.

What she didn't understand was the transformation. Who was this guy who was James Bond cool tonight? He'd always hated these pretentious and elite functions. Man, the number of times she'd listened to him lecture her. A spark of irritation flared. Hadn't he accused her of being shallow because she mixed with this crowd? It looked like he was doing a great job of enjoying himself. It bugged her that he seemed to fit in, and he did it well.

A part of her missed his tussled locks and ripped, blue jeans. A lump formed in her throat. He'd had his chance. Actually, he'd had more than one. She missed the idea of him, but the reality had been too harsh.

"Darling, is that your second drink? Best slow down, petal, there's a whole night ahead." Inez leaned in and kissed her on each cheek.

She wouldn't tell Inez she was already on her third.

Sophie's whole heart opened up at the sight of her boss, and she returned the kiss. Inez wore a pure white suit worn backwards with the opening of the jacket displaying her smooth back. The collar sat at the base of Inez's throat but a dazzling long gold-link chain with baubles at discrete intervals ran down her back. There was a perfectly ironed and crisp seam down the middle of each leg.

In contrast to the stark white outfit, she wore shiny black patent leather shoes. Her hair was pulled away from her face and large earrings matched the necklace. Like the models she hired, Inez looked incredible.

In spite of her boss's advice Sophie took another large sip of the drink and continued to watch Max.

Inez followed her gaze. "Hm, he's a dish. If I liked men, I'd wish he was my supper," she said and giggled. Inez made the most outrageously inappropriate comments.

"That's Max."

Inez turned between her and the man across the room. "The Max?" she asked.

Sophie nodded.

"Simone is draped all over him. Let's fix that." Before Sophie could tell her not to bother, Inez strode across the room.

Caught off guard, Sophie walked three steps behind and arrived after Inez had ordered Simone to mingle and sell a few handbags. She was the boss, and Simone took off.

"Max," Sophie said, getting his attention, "this is Inez, my boss and the CEO of Lilly Malone." Inez leaned in for a kiss as Max held out his hand.

"It's a pleasure to meet you," he said gazing down at Inez's hand that held onto his for too long.

"Max. This piece is beautiful." Sophie indicated the vase.

"Did you make it, darling?" Inez moved closer.

"Yes. It's one of my latest. At the risk of sounding a bit like a wanker, I love it." He gazed at it with adoration.

"What's it doing here, Max?"

"Well, it's the main donation in tonight's auction. It's a long story, but I've been doing some work for Francis Creations, a photographic company..."

"A photographer?"

"Yeah, but I'm not a photographer, obviously. I've been doing their bookkeeping on a part-time basis. I've gotten to know them and they're fantastic to work for. Anyway, they've donated a framed photograph and some free sessions for the auction, and they asked me if I'd like to donate one of my works. It's such a worthwhile charity, and well, this is where you work and I thought, well, I don't know..." His words petered out before he said, "So, here it is."

"Let me get this straight," Inez questioned him. "You created this and have other pieces?" Her hand was to her chin in contemplation. "I recall Sophie mentioned you were an artist. I think this is exquisite. I would like to commission you for a piece for my home and also one for our main reception area at Lilly Malone, and a smaller version for each of our consulting rooms. How many do we have, Sophie?"

Sophie counted on her fingers, "Six, I think."

"Okay, that's two large vases and six smaller ones. Anything like this one and I'll be delighted. Okay?"

"Are you serious?" Sophie asked incredulous.

"I'm deadly serious, dear. I don't joke about such matters. What's the name of this creation, Max?"

Max shuffled his feet and hung his head. They both waited.

"Sofia Gabrielle," he answered in a whisper. Inez raised her eyebrows and looked at Sophie. Sophie's chest tightened and she sipped her drink because she didn't know what else to do.

"I want you two announcing the highest bidder later. Max, you can tell everyone about your inspiration for the work."

"What. No," Sophie exclaimed.

Inez's eyes twinkled, "Okay, agreed that might be embarrassing."

Inez glided away to do what she did best: mingle, talk and sell the quality of Lilly Malone to all in her path.

With hot cheeks, Sophie ignored Max's confession. She was probably getting ahead of herself anyway. There could be a million reasons for that name.

"That's fantastic about the company. How did you get involved doing their books?"

Max looked at the floor and rubbed the toe of his shoe before answering.

"Strangely, it dropped into my lap. Literally. The day at the markets was one of my miserable attempts to drum up some business and, of course, make some money. It wasn't a good idea. I've learned that lesson. Anyway, at the end of the day, this man threw his newspaper on my table and fortuitously, an ad stared up at me. It was for a bookkeeper and it got me thinking. Those things you said were true. I was too stubborn to realise it. I was desperate for my dreams of being an artist to come true, and I had to make it happen to prove my parents wrong. I struggled to accept it wasn't working to plan. That was hard, and it took me awhile to face reality. I applied for the part-time position from the paper and then they recommended me to *Francis Creations*. It's snowballed from there. I have some regular work and more importantly a steady income, but still plenty of time to create."

"That's amazing. Well done. I know it must've been difficult to compromise. But look at this, it's one of your best, so something is working."

"I had endless inspiration." He stared at her with his stormy eyes.

Okay, maybe she couldn't ignore the sculpture's name, and how she still felt about him.

The music began to pump and the room came alive. People started dancing.

"Do you think we can talk? I need to apologise. Can we grab a drink and go outside or do you need to work?"

"No, we can leave. I'm more of a guest tonight too."

Max gave her a quizzical look and placed his hand to her back. Her dress frilled across her shoulders but left them bare. The skirt fell to above her ankles and for once, her dress made her feel like a princess.

Max's hand scorched her back. His touch. That heat. It made her skin sizzle. He was like a permanent hot water bottle to her cool skin. She paused and looked at him waiting for his reaction. He didn't comment but his hand didn't more from that spot.

Chapter Twenty-Five

They were almost at the door to the terrace when Sophie saw Max stiffen. He stumbled, and Sophie put her hand to his back to prevent them from colliding.

They'd walked the short distance across the dance floor in silence and Sophie trailed slightly behind him as they moved through the crowd. As they neared the outdoor area, the cool air of the summer evening drifted inside and made her body temperature dip. She shivered.

"Mother," she heard Max say. She closed the gap and stood beside him and sure enough, there was Mrs Cartwright, and presumably her husband who Sophie had never met.

"Mrs Cartwright you look amazing. That dress is the perfect style and colour for you." The words were out before Sophie could stop them.

"Sophie,' Max growled at her.

"No, that's not sales talk. You really do look stunning, and not simply because you're wearing one of the Lilly Malone dresses I chose as part of your collection."

Max gazed at the ground. Okay, best if she shut up. Mrs Cartwright was an example of a client well-serviced. The outfit was perfect. To be honest, Sophie was kind of chuffed.

'Thank you, Sophie. You always did have a way with words."

Huh, Sophie wasn't sure that was a compliment. Mrs Cartwright continued, "This is my husband and Max's father, Frank."

They exchanged introductions. Max paused for a moment too long.

"What are you doing here?' he finally asked.

It was Frank who said, "You made it into one of these fancy art magazines your mother subscribes to." Frank held it up and Max snatched it out of his hands to take a better look.

There was a one-page photo of Max in a clean studio and looking like a fashion model in a collared polo and slacks. On the adjoining page there seemed to be a question and answer with him and a few select shots of his most recent pieces.

"It's a fabulous article and provides incredible exposure. I was showing the ladies at lunch the other day and they all wanted me to place orders for them. I, of course, informed them that I am not my son's personal secretary and they would need to contact you directly," Mrs Cartwright said.

Phew, what a relief. For a moment Sophie wondered who this woman was but the snarky comment at the end saved her. Still the cold and proper Mrs Cartwright. But, but… Sophie looked at Max. She could tell he was thinking exactly the same thing. She noticed he bit the inside of his lip. She'd bet he was struggling not to bite his tongue.

Sophie placed her arm into the corner of his elbow so they stood close. "That's brilliant. What a great feature. I'm sure you'll have an avalanche of new orders now."

Max appeared to be collecting his thoughts. He stared at his mother. His mother returned the glare. Which way would this go?

"Thanks, Dad, for bringing it along. I hadn't seen the article. I spoke to them weeks ago and wasn't sure if they'd even run it. This is going to help bring in new clients. I'm really excited." He smiled his brightest smile as his long fringe flopped into his face.

God, he was adorable, and Sophie gripped his arm tighter never wanting to let him go.

"Look at this," his father exclaimed excitedly. "These are all the bids we've made in the silent auction tonight. Your mother is determined that the beautiful vase you've created is coming home with us."

It was obvious Max's father was saying all the things his mother could not, or perhaps refused to. As long as they were her sentiments, it didn't matter.

"What? Mum, Dad, that's crazy. I can make any piece you like. You don't need to bid."

"Well perhaps you can design something original for us for the house. A one-off special piece. I would really like that," his mother said.

"Me, too," Max replied, his voice quiet and soft. He looked at his mother when he spoke. "I'll start thinking of ideas straight away." His mother glanced away first. Some things would take time.

"Sophie, thank you for the shoes and the designs. It's all beautiful. I do think it's best I stick with the lovely young girl your CEO has assigned me. No conflict of interest then."

"Sure, Mrs Cartwright. I'm pleased that you're happy with the label and will stick with us."

She nodded.

Another couple attracted his parent's attention and they engaged in small talk with them.

"We'll see you later," Max said.

Sophie steered him outside quickly. She wanted to squeal.

They sat in a far away in a dimly lit corner of the terrace. The rumble of music and animated voices drifted out followed by the frequent chime of a pokie machine indicating a win followed by the tumble of coins.

The sky had turned midnight blue and stars sprinkled the sky. Max sat so close their legs touched.

"Don't get too excited," he said, "but yes, it's a start. That's probably as soft and kind as mother will ever get. I haven't had that for years. I can thank the magazine. External affirmation means she sees me becoming successful. That's when she'll be proud of me, not before. But that's okay."

"It's fantastic," Sophie shrieked too loudly.

Max grinned and said, "So why aren't you working tonight? Are you still employed by Lilly Malone?"

His focus was intense. His eyes had been one of the first things she'd noticed about him. The first part of him she was attracted to. They were expressive and darkened with emotion.

She'd paused too long. Max said, "Your job? Tell me about your job."

"How do you know about my job?"

Max laughed and placed a hand on her knee. "I don't. I'm not sure what you're talking about. I was asking about Lilly Malone."

"Oh, sorry. Gosh, you won't believe it. I know Gaby blurted out that night that I have an interest in art, well more than an interest. It's been a long-term dream of mine. Anyway, I had a bit of a meltdown after I yelled at your mother. I was in serious trouble with Inez and risked losing my job. I panicked. But what came out of that is that I told Inez about my personal circumstances."

"Hang on. Your boss didn't know you cared for your sister?" Max shook his head. "And you say I'm stubborn."

"Yeah, I know, right. But I actually don't recall saying that."

"That's what you meant."

"Am I telling this story, or not?" She rolled her eyes.

"Anyway, Inez has been incredibly supportive since she found out, and coincidentally, her girlfriend works for the museum and has helped me get a job. I mean I still had to apply and be interviewed and all that, but she introduced me to all the right people."

"What? That's amazing. So no more Lilly Malone?" He appeared puzzled.

"Max," Sophie said seriously. "As a struggling artist, you understand that art doesn't pay, right?"

He nodded.

"It's a junior position. I assist with small exhibitions and help out with anything. Even the coffee shop. But there's hope for more. There's a succession plan, so Evelyn, that's Inez's girlfriend, she'll move into the principal curator position once that fellow retires and cross fingers, I might take over her job." Sophie squealed. "Or I could be getting ahead of myself. There're others before me. But anyway, because my position at the moment pays peanuts, I'm still styling for Lilly, but for not as many clients. I'm here tonight sot of working, but mostly not."

"That's fabulous. I'm so happy for you. It's your dream come true. Even though I'm not sure how you're managing two jobs. But you were always good at juggling." He stopped talking and smiled.

Sophie's stomach did a funny flip.

"I wasn't sure I'd see you again," Max murmured close to her ear. He moved back an inch, but his voice was husky and deep. "I'm seriously so happy for you. Small steps to a bigger goal. That's something you've done right. I jumped ahead of myself."

Sophie's chest heaved at the timbre of his voice. It dripped down her throat like melting honey. Oh boy, she'd love to coat herself in it. She focused on the stars behind Max's head because his lips were only inches away from hers. If her boobs weren't safely encased in her dress they'd be jumping right out to attention.

"Tell me about the vase. Why did you name it after Gaby and me?"

"Isn't it obvious?" Max paused, gazed at her, and then whispered, "I love you, Sophie." He glanced down at his hands before returning to look into her eyes.

Her breath seemed stuck in her chest but she couldn't pull her gaze away from his stare. The intensity she adored was back and it was directed at her.

"I've been such an idiot. When we met I was angry, stuck and unhappy. You made me see things differently. Perhaps some of the trouble was my entitled upbringing. I expected things to fall in my lap. Well, in fairness, they had most of my childhood. I hadn't learnt the strategies to cope or strive or problem-solve. And then, of course, there's you and that was your entire life. Dealing with one dilemma to the next both in your personal life at and work.

"You're the example I've been living by. Because of you, I'm heading where I need to go. Thank you for making me realise it, which forced me to see things more clearly. Without you, I'd probably be stomping around poor, hungry, and angry at the world."

Okay. She'd melted, and all that was left was the pink chiffon dress.

"I've been an idiot too. I was just as stubborn," she admitted. "I thought I could handle everything life had to throw at me while caring for my sister. I was determined to manage alone. Too scared to ask people for help. Frightened they would think I couldn't cope. We've both made mistakes."

She turned sideways on the lounge and gripped his hands in hers. "I love you, too, Max. I'll believe in you, and you'll believe in me. We'll have each other's backs and we'll try not make silly mistakes anymore. You're talented and you'll make it, and art can become your entire life. Perhaps not straight away, but you'll make a success of the life you've chosen. I'm certain of it." She squeezed his fingers. "As for me, for the first time ever I'm seeing a future doing work I love and enough money to care for my sister without constant stress. I'm sorry for walking away. I should have hung by you, and helped. I really want to be with you. Can we agree that we'll stand by each other?"

Max nodded as he moved closer.

Sophie focused on his handsome face as he leaned in and their lips touched. Fireworks exploded and echoed a distant rumble in the sky.

Nothing could distract her from their kiss. His full lips pressed against her mouth and his tongue swept out to lick her lips, and then his teeth nipped at her bottom lip. Another kaleidoscope of colour hit the sky and he pulled away. Immediately Sophie felt cold.

Max must've seen her shiver. He draped his arm over her bare shoulders and one finger caressed her upper arm. The sensation rocked her right down to her core. Neither spoke as they started at the brightly lit sky and the pinwheels of vivid shades.

"Hey, you two. See those fireworks. They're amazing," Gaby called, her oval face beaming. "Max, I'm so glad you made Sophie understand. You two are meant to be together. No more moods, okay." She placed a hand on Max's shoulder.

"You're a smart girl, Gaby." Max replied. "But you know what, I think the future will be fine now because I have everything I need." He tugged Gaby toward them until she toppled into their huddle and together with their heads held high, they laughed as the finale of fireworks shattered the sky.

"What's this?" he said to Gaby pointing to her clothes. "Is that a work uniform?"

Gaby bounced on her feet and said, "Yep. Uh huh. Can you believe it? If you come down to the café on Coventry Street I might make you an iced latte, or whatever you like. Maybe even serve it with a muffin or a slice of cake."

Max pulled her in for another embrace. "That's awesome. You'll be fabulous there. That smile will dazzle all of the customers."

Behind her a young man stood awkwardly. He was dressed in the similar attire of black shirt and jeans.

Gaby tugged his arm and pulled him forward. "This is Tristian. He works at the café with me. He's the boss's son, but we won't hold that against him. I invited him along. I hope that's okay? Plus, I didn't want to be the only loser here in hospitality gear. They might mistake me for staff."

Sophie didn't think it was possible for her heart to swell any further.

She smiled at the shy young man. "Tristan, it's really lovely to meet you. I'm glad you could come. It's a dull adult affair I'm afraid, and despite telling our friend Inez that Gaby would be bored, she insisted she come. Inez is trying to make an adult out of her too soon. Make sure you have a drink. An apple juice that is," she emphasised, "and enjoy yourself."

"Did I hear my name?"

A flash of light hit them as Inez took a round of photos with her phone. She moved poor young Tristan into the frame even though he was quietly trying to edge farther away.

"Inez, this is Gaby's friend, Tristan," Sophie introduced them.

Inez rolled her eyes. "I know, darling, we met inside. Plus, I know Tristan from the café. He makes the most wonderful coffee and sometimes, if I'm ever so good, he gives me a dash of something special." She winked at the boy and his cheeks flushed.

Inez moved closer to young couple. "Adorable," she uttered as she pinched them both on the cheeks before blinding the pair with another photograph.

"So sweet," she murmured. Evelyn appeared behind her embracing Inez around the middle with her two arms and squeezing tight. Inez placed one hand over hers and showed Evelyn the images.

"Aha," she exclaimed, "it's time to announce the winners of the auction. C'mon young lady." She grabbed Gaby's arm. "You come too, Tristan. You need to see the inspiration for Max's latest work. There's the most exquisite piece inside he's donated. You simply must see it before someone snaps it up for a squillion dollars."

Inez moved away but stopped and turned to look back over her shoulder.

"Max, Sophie, you're on."

Max leaned over and kissed her one last time before they went inside.

She didn't think she'd ever tire of the feel of those luscious lips on hers.

ABOUT THE AUTHOR

Leanne is a lawyer and author who loves romance and reading. Her law career has caused her addiction to coffee, but provides her with countless story ideas. She lives in Brisbane, Australia with her husband and three children.

Connect with Leanne:
website: leannelovegroveauthor.com
Instagram: @leannelovegroveauthor
facebook: @leannelovegroveauthor
twitter: @leannelovegroveauthor

www.BOROUGHSPUBLISHINGGROUP.com

If you enjoyed this book, please write a review. Our authors appreciate the feedback, and it helps future readers find books they love. We welcome your comments and invite you to send them to info@boroughspublishinggroup.com. Follow us on Facebook, Twitter and Instagram, and be sure to sign up for our newsletter for surprises and new releases from your favorite authors.

Are you an aspiring writer? Check out www.boroughspublishinggroup.com/submit and see if we can help you make your dreams come true.